THE Penny Scam

L.H. WILLIAMS

About the Authors

Dear Reader,

If you've read our first book, *Saving Dee*, you already know that L. H. Williams is a pseudonym for Louise and Heyward Williams. We are a young-at-heart married couple who found each other again after many years apart. Right away we discovered a shared love of writing that began more than fifty years ago in junior high school when we studied English with our much-loved teacher, Doris Pock. We recently traveled to Albany, New York, and had lunch with her. Much to our delight, she declared *Saving Dee*, to be "a romp." We love her for that!

In fact, over the years Heyward and I have been avid readers. I love Regency Romance, and Heyward usually reaches for the adventure books. When we decided to write, we thought we should have some fun with it. So, if you find our characters and our plots to be somewhat "over the top," you're right. Our heroines are beautiful, our heroes rich AND handsome, and our crooks and bad guys are downright dirty dogs, but they always manage to screw up! That's the way we like it.

We are having fun writing, and we hope you have enjoy reading *The Penny Scam,* the second book of "The Dee Chronicles." While it continues the story of Dee and Jared, it also adds some new characters, including "DJ" – the quirky computer hacker turned hero of this sometimes wacky novel. Full of plot twists and turns, and some hijinks, this book will give you your "Dee fix," as one of our readers recently wrote to us.

Meanwhile, we are hard at work on our third book, entitled

Lady in Lace, which refers to a valuable last-century Italian oil painting that's featured in our story.

All the best,
Louise and Heyward Williams

Email: TheDeeChronicles@gmail.com
Twitter: @SunlandLouise

Prologue

THERE WAS A QUIET CHIME, but Ellen and Irving were too busy to hear it. Subconsciously they recorded it, but right now Ellen was astride Irving's recumbent body, gasping for joy. She was riding like an equestrienne at dressage, and when they came to the final gate, they went over it together. And then collapsed in victorious rapture.

When their breathing slowed, and he recovered after a sniff from his inhaler, they looked at each other.

"Was there a…did we have a…" she whispered a little hoarsely.

"I think so," he said, gasping for breath.

Without another word, she unwound her voluptuous form from his gnome-like body and kissed him passionately. Whatever Irving lacked in physical beauty was made up for in the dimension of his "love wand," as Ellen affectionately called it.

They padded naked into their home office and logged onto their computers.

"Oh my, it's XhumeMe," she said. "Remember him?"

"I thought he was still in cyber jail," he answered. "Look at this. He's trying to hack into us."

Ellen's fingers tapped on her keyboard. "He already has. At least he's passed the first level. I've blocked him from going any further."

"I wonder what he wants."

Her fingers flew over her keyboard again.

"He wants us!"

Chapter 1

Smooth Sailing

DEE AND JARED WERE SAILING his wooden ketch, *Chauffeuse*, north from Fort Lauderdale in the early morning with a good southwest wind, fair skies, and light seas. Their plan was to take her as far north as time permitted and then Jared would call his crew to take her home for the winter. Although Dee hadn't had any sailing experience, she was a quick learner and he enjoyed teaching her. In the short time they had known each other they had experienced a piratical kidnapping of Dee, a rescue by Jared, and the financial ruin of her criminal husband, Steve, who had to divorce her in Las Vegas as a result. Best of all, Dee and Jared had fallen in love.

He relaxed at the wheel and said, "Once we get into the Gulf Stream, we'll make good time. Did you know that Benjamin Franklin was the one who officially charted it? Anyway, we'll go as far as we can until we run out of coffee and then put into shore. I've heard of a little yard in Norfolk that specializes in restoring wooden boats. It's also in financial trouble, so I'd like to stop there and have a look around. Maybe they can help this lady go a little faster."

"You never stop, do you?" she asked.

"That's what life is all about," he answered.

———

They sailed for a while in quiet companionship until Dee looked around and realized they were out of sight of land. While this gave her some qualms, she also realized there were no other boats in sight. A sly twinkle came into her eyes as she reached for the strings holding her bikini top.

"I wondered when you were going to do that," she heard Jared say. "Just remember to put sunscreen on the parts that don't normally see the light of day."

He was steering with his toes, and she thought he looked so relaxed and peaceful. Her love for him surged in her heart. She dropped the rest of her bikini and came to sit beside him.

"Isn't there an autopilot here somewhere?" she asked.

He smiled and turned it on.

Afterward, when Dee had the wheel, she reveled in the feel of the wind in the sails and the gentle rise and fall of the sea under her bare feet. Jared sat on the cushions in the cockpit and watched her.

"Wind's coming around," he eventually said. "Time to trim the sails a little or bear off half a point."

She looked at the chart. "We could use a little more sea room off this coast; I think I'll bear away." Then she looked at the telltale at the masthead to gauge the wind direction, then at the wind catspaws on the water, and then at the compass in front of the wheel.

"Half a point should do it," she said.

He smiled in agreement. They shared the silence of sailing the blue water and their own thoughts for another hour.

"Do you know what I miss most?" she asked, and then continued before Jared could answer. "It's working in the art gallery in New York. I made it a mecca for so many wonderful people. I knew how to help the indecisive ones choose the right piece and how to sell overpriced art to customers like my ex-husband. But my real joy was working with the customers who knew and loved art."

She looked at Jared and saw him smiling in agreement.

"They would ask me to find a special piece, and I got to know their tastes and worked hard for them. My favorites were the art lovers who asked me to discover and develop emerging artists. They would look at examples of their paintings and say yea or nay. Three of these aficionados knew each other and would bid on who would be the one to sponsor them." She paused. "I was so happy doing that and I was good at it. But Steve made me give it all up. That's what I miss."

Her voice trailed off. He sat silent as she thought for a while.

"If only I could get that back. I've heard that my old gallery isn't doing well. The tyrant manager who was once my boss resurfaced and bought the place. The staff hates him, so he can't keep his employees for very long."

She looked at him, knowing he'd been listening carefully, but now she noticed he was grinning at her.

"Wait a minute, Jared, you turn around businesses for fun. Can't you do something?"

"I could if I wanted to, but I'd have to know who owned it," he said, almost as if he were teasing her.

She bit her tongue. She wanted to ask him to buy the gallery for her, but she was too proud to ask. He'd done so much for her already.

"Why don't you buy it yourself?" he asked.

She looked at him incredulously. "With what?" she joked, "My good looks?"

He was still smiling.

"Oh, and if I know Steve, when you got him to sign the divorce papers, he left me with nothing."

His smile broadened, as though he was carrying a secret. "Actually, Dee, I need to tell you something. We knew Steve was in over his head in dirty dealings, so we had to catch him. When our sting went down at the Bellagio, we stripped him of the cash he was holding in accounts he'd already created in your name and we transferred those funds to a new account. You are now worth a little over two million dollars, my love. Don't spend it all in one place."

She was speechless; she looked at him wide-eyed. Then it started to sink in. He had not only—she remembered his word— 'extricated' her from her marriage to Steve, but he had also ruined Steve's business. And, somehow, he had transferred some of Steve's wealth to her.

"Watch your luff," he said. Her head came up and she hastily corrected course. It took another hour at the helm for her to mentally sort out all she had learned. More than that, it gave her time to consider the possibilities.

He reached over and took the helm. "The gallery is yours if you want it. I've already asked my New York law firm to look into it. It's going cheap because, as you said, that tyrant is running it into the ground."

"You mean I can buy it, own it, and get my old clients back?"

"Yes, but you'll have to work at the last part. Anything you want to do, you can do; your life is yours now, Dee."

"I owe you so much, my darling."

"No, I owe *you* for making me believe in love again. He turned to look at her and held her gaze. "Dee, I don't want to waste another minute. I know what I want, but I want to know if you want it too. Dee, will you marry me?"

There was no hesitation; she had already felt the wind in her sails and the compass direction for her life.

"You knew the answer to that question before you asked it," she said, turning back to view the luff of the jib. "But for the record, the answer is yes!"

Chapter 2

The Debriefing

MELANIE WAS A CALIFORNIA GIRL by heart, but these days Washington, DC was the center of her world. It was where she and Mitch shared a cozy townhouse while they awaited the birth of their son. She had a busy day of meetings ahead of her, but she took a moment to reminisce about how it had all come about.

It was a windy Sunday morning on a beach in San Diego about five years ago. Thirty or so masochists were gearing up for a five-mile open water race – just to keep fit! By the end of the race four people hauled themselves out of the water at almost the same time, but there could be only one winner – and that was Jared Herreshoff. The other two men were Mitch and Mark. She knew that Mark had his eye on her, but it was Mitch who had finally won her heart. She'd introduced herself, they'd all gone out for a beer, and a security business was born. Thinking back, Melanie was amazed at how bold she'd been – telling them she could pull this off because she had "a degree from Caltech, and was her daddy's daughter." More than anything, it was her own courage and belief in herself that had grown this business.

Today she was debriefing everyone who had participated in the takedown of Steve Milan in Las Vegas. She began with Ellen and

Irving – that is, when she could get their attention. They acted like a couple of teenagers who had surrendered their virginity to each other in the back seat of a '57 Chevy after the senior prom. In a way it was true, but Melanie didn't know that. What she did know was that sending them out in the field had changed their lives. For two people who had barely acknowledged each other before, they were now looking longingly into each other's eyes, as if they were unaware of the world around them.

"If I can get your attention!" commanded Melanie. After all, she was the CEO of Protek, the security company they worked for. While they didn't exactly snap and salute, they did get the message. "What did you learn on this field op?" The two of them, along with several others, had recently returned from Las Vegas, where they had carried out a sting operation on Steve Milan, a small-time criminal who owned an import-export business that specialized in shady deals. The man's lovely wife, the unwitting victim, Dee, was now under the protection of Jared Herreshoff, Protek's owner.

Irving and Ellen looked at each other; Ellen spoke first. "I once called Mitch and Mark knuckle draggers until I saw what it was like to go one-on-one with them. I owe them a serious apology. At the casino, Mark was there looking like a bodyguard, and Mitch was disguised as Dee's aging husband. But I've seen him work out. He could have killed with his bare hands if anyone had threatened her. In a heartbeat. Before Mark could have even drawn his gun! And yet these two scary men are so polite when we meet them in the office. I had no idea how good, no, how powerful, they were. I'm glad they're on our side."

"I'm pleased you saw that," said Melanie. "That's why I selected you two for the job. You're going to be working with them again. I want to expand the business and Jared has agreed. Irving, what are your thoughts on the table odds?"

"Oh shit," blurted out Irving. "With Patsy pushing the

wheel and Ellen and me calculating the probabilities, we could have broken the house. Instead we made it look like a run of good luck. That's how we drew Steve in." Melanie kept nodding, pleased with his analysis. "As it was, Dee's 'ex' lost his shirt," he continued, "which is how we planned it. Ellen, Mark, Mitch, Karen, and I made a tidy sum, and we've heard Jared's going to let us keep it. But unless you want us to run this game again, we should—um—offer to show the casinos how it's done. And more important, how to prevent it. I hate to admit it, but there are folks out there who are just as smart as we are."

"That's exactly what this new project is all about," said Melanie. "Trent, head of security at the Bellagio, thought he had seen it all until you two showed up. He was amazed. He had a long talk with Jared after you returned, and they reached an agreement. Protek is going to consult for them and you two are going back to Las Vegas to meet with Trent. As a pair of amateurs in the gambling arena, you blew him away. He couldn't even see how you were doing it. He also has some tricks to show you, so you will be undergoing a crash course in cheating at casino gambling. You'll meet people who learned to deal seconds when they were five years old, and those who know how to slide bets at the last moment before the wheel stops. And on and on."

Ellen and Irving looked at each other and their eyes seemed to focus. "I can be the front," said Ellen finally, "but Irving's the star if you want this to happen."

Now it was Melanie's turn to look puzzled.

"Do it, lover," cooed Ellen.

Irving produced a deck of cards, and with elegant hand movements, he showed it to Melanie, riffling it one-handed in a face-up arc to show her that it was all there. Then he scooped it up, also one-handed, and shuffled it twice. He showed it to Melanie again and turned it over. The two of spades was on the bottom. He showed her the top card: the two of clubs. He shuffled it again and dealt from the top. Melanie had all four aces in front of her. Then he showed her the top card on the deck. It was the two of spades.

"I can't imagine what happened to the two of clubs," said Melanie.

Irving turned over the deck.

The next interview didn't go as well. Edgar had reverted to his former self and showed up in a soiled T-shirt and basketball shorts, looking generally unhygienic. Melanie gave him a long, hard stare. She had hired him because he was a brilliant mathematician with a minor in computer technology, but in the field, he had shown that he was still an adolescent. *What a waste. He could have been so successful.*

"Edgar, you're fired," she said. "Security will escort you out. All personal items in your cube will be delivered to your residence. Your office computers are being reformatted as we speak. Do not ask me to give you a reference, because you don't deserve one. You endangered your fellow employees with your behavior. There are no second chances in the security business."

At first, he didn't believe her. But then, he'd smoked a joint before lunch, so he was still a little hazy. "Okay," he said. "No problem, I can always get another job."

She stared him down. She had already put the news out on the street about him: "Don't touch this guy with a ten-foot pole."

When he stood to leave, Mark stepped in to escort him out.

"That serious?" Edgar asked.

Mark was silent.

Melanie was tired. In her sixth month of pregnancy, she knew this kind of executive hardball was wearing on her, and she desperately needed some time to relax. But the next debrief was the easiest and then she could leave early and go home to Mitch, who would have her tomato juice (which used to be a Bloody Mary) ready for her and would hold her in his arms on the couch.

She called Karen into her office, sensing the younger woman's apprehension as she walked in. She realized Karen had probably seen Mark escort Edgar out, so she moved quickly to put her mind at ease.

"You did exceptionally well in Vegas, as did Ellen and Irving. Edgar was a disappointment. You figured him out and turned him off before he could damage the company."

She saw that Karen was beginning to relax.

"You are an intelligent lady; I watched you recalculating Irving and Ellen's bets when they were taking Steve Milan down. Jared says to tell you that what you won is yours, free and clear."

Karen's face lit up. Melanie was fully aware that what she'd won that night was well into six figures.

"Now, here's your next assignment: you'll be going back to Vegas with Ellen and Irving to work with Trent on our new business venture, and you will be its vice president. It's all about stopping, or at least cutting down on the amount of cheating that goes on in his casino. You will spend a month there in training and then report back to me here. If I think you are ready (and I have already made up my mind, so don't screw up) you will sit at this desk while I am popping Mitch's baby. I will then be back after my maternity leave. Then you will be in charge of Ellen and Irving and that whole new line of the business. You will, of course, have all of our resources at your disposal, including, if necessary, the heavyweights.

"Mark and Mitch?" Karen asked.

Melanie looked at her and smiled a wicked smile. "Only Mark," she said, "Mitch is all mine!"

From Karen's expression, that was fine with her.

"One more thing," said Melanie. "Find out how Irving shuffles those cards!"

Karen quirked an eyebrow in confusion. Obviously, she had yet to find out what Melanie was talking about.

Chapter 3

DJ's Confession

DAVID JESSE OWEN, KNOWN AS DJ, aka "XhumeMe," lit
a cigarette from the one he was snuffing out and went
back to work on his laptop. He thought the name was
clever because it meant "Dig Me Up," as if anyone could find out
who he really was. He was wrong. Surrounded by empty takeout
containers and dirty ashtrays, he was so far removed from the
way he was brought up that he was almost unrecognizable. But
that didn't bother him—all he cared about was the flickering
screen in front of him.

He thought of himself as a modern-day Robin Hood, although
he was, by trade, a hacker, and a very successful one at that. But
what set him apart from the other hackers was what he called
"his gift." He looked around the room at the pictures of his little
sister Lisa—lost to him forever when he was ten and she was
only six. He remembered how she always sat propped up in her
tiny wheelchair and how devastated he had been when she died.
So, his gift to Lisa came in the form of anonymous donations
to any children's charity he could think of. Some of his ideas
came from watching television. He'd already adopted numerous
orphan girls in Africa and Central America and had sent funds
to local children's hospitals; when they asked for a donor's name,
if he wrote anything it was always "for my darling Lisa."

It started out small, but as his hacking activities increased, so
did his charitable giving. He was making huge amounts of money
for his clients, and the "gift skim" was by now becoming quite

large. It was the latest gossip in charitable circles. He hacked into the charitable foundations and made large donations. In fact, at one recent luncheon, representatives of five out of six local charities reported discovering anonymous deposits in their bank accounts—one contribution topped fifty thousand dollars.

He stopped working long enough to scan the computers on the tables and desks in his living room, which was his makeshift office. One monitor was running an endless stream of numbers, programmed as it was to find the password he needed to get into one of his client's accounts. This one was attached to a vintage Cray he'd purchased at a surplus sale for $9,600 —down from the $8.8 million it had cost the government in 1976. It looked like two fifty-five gallon drums stacked on top of each other. Although it ran at a fraction of the bus speed of modern desktops, it was the first really powerful parallel processing computer. In fact, the reason for its shape was to minimize the time delay on the wires between the processors. In the back was a slot for maintenance access.

DJ's friends told him that the pie-shaped wedge looked like the back of a prom dress when you unzipped it after the prom in the back seat of your dad's car. He couldn't really visualize this since he'd never been to a prom, much less in a back seat with a willing lady, but he took them at their word. Around the outside at the base was a set of cushions that looked like a curved sofa. They housed the power supplies. He used to sit there and think he could hear it computing. Actually, it was the hum of the cooling system. He knew that but didn't care; to him it was alive.

He had installed the Cray in the basement of his apartment building with the help of his friend, the super. He'd made some modifications to the hardware and had rewritten the operating system to focus on what he needed it to do—and now it was a priceless addition to his computer collection.

Because DJ's apartment building once housed a machine

shop, it had the power input needed for this dinosaur. A friend who moonlighted as a plumber helped him redesign the refrigeration system to replace the original Freon design with a more "environmentally friendly" system. It not only cooled the computer, but, in winter, it directed the heat to all of the other apartments, so the residents began to notice that their heating bills were almost nonexistent. In the summer the system reversed, and since it was much more efficient, there was enough capacity to cool the entire building. The other residents thought DJ was a little weird, but when they saw how much money they were saving, they shook their heads and let him be. He could have hacked into the power company and deleted all of their accounts, but instead he religiously logged in and paid them online—with funds from companies and clients who had stolen the money in the first place. He thought they wouldn't miss it.

Another PC was generating an inordinate amount of email, a strange mixture of junk mail and requests from clients for updates to their activities. It sorted and deleted it at an unbelievable rate. This algorithm had taken him almost a month to write and he thought about selling the rights to Microsoft, but by that time he didn't need the money. Two laptops were devoted to bank accounts, so he could track the progress of both his clients' accounts and his own.

The emails from his key clients generated a special bell, which kept ringing with an insistence he could no longer overlook. It was beginning to annoy him, so he turned his attention in that direction.

The most recent one read: "DJ. Get yr head out of yr ass! Again yr short with our profits money of this operations. Find leak and fix it. If we haf to find it for you, you will be expired."

Oops! DJ decided these messages were getting harder and harder to ignore. Maybe it was time he sought help—before he got "expired."

He thought idly that he was way too young for that.

<hr>

As Ellen and Irving stood half-naked over the blinking computer screen, another one of their monitors came alive—with a Skype request. Ellen dove for a towel, but it was too late. DJ was already staring at her breasts, and for a second he couldn't seem to speak. But a worried look soon crossed his face and he finally sputtered out what he had to say.

"Where have you two *been*?" he all but howled into his speaker.

Ellen choked back a giggle. "Why you little pipsqueak, DJ. How did you find us? I haven't seen you since I gave that jobs seminar to your high school in Newark. God, that has to be what, six, seven years ago now?"

"Eight," he said, now stony faced.

"Give me a minute, hon, and let me put some clothes on, okay? Keep your pants on, fella."

She could see DJ was rapidly losing his cool, so she tapped Irving on the shoulder and told him to get up off the floor and keep DJ busy until she could find her wrap. By the time she wandered back into their computer room, she could see DJ and Irving were deep in conversation, and Irving was all ears. DJ was spilling the beans, and Irving was all but taking notes, he was so interested.

"Okay, kid," said Irving. "Yes, you were right to come to us, and yes, we are the best. But you've got yourself into a bit of a pickle—considering the types you're working with—no, working for. But I think we can help you. Not over the wires, obviously. We'll have to come in person."

Irving motioned for Ellen to take notes. They'd fly in to Newark Airport, then take a taxi to a coffee shop in a tough part of town. "Tomorrow, kid." We'll call your cell phone when we land, okay? And keep your shirt on until then, right?"

Both screens went dark. Ellen cooed into Irving's ear, "Would you like some scrambled eggs, honey? After all, you gotta keep your strength up, right?"

Chapter 4

Stormy Seas

EE AND JARED SAILED INTO a brilliant sunset. She was still at the helm while he made a delicious dinner of shellfish bouillabaisse with lobster, clams, shrimp, mussels, and saffron in the stock. They ate from large soup bowls as they sat on deck while *Chauffeuse* sailed happily along. Dee cleaned up and then Jared sent her below to get some sleep. A day frolicking in the sun had made her drowsy; she asked him what he was going to do.

"Sail," he said, "and make sure we don't run into anything hard. Now get some sleep; you're going to take the middle watch."

"What's the middle watch?"

"Midnight to four a.m."

"What?"

"Don't worry. I'll sleep on deck, so if you need me I'll be there. It's time you became a real sailor."

"Oh," she said in a small voice. The implications of what this meant reached her. She went below and stretched out on their berth thinking that...she would...never fall...aslee...

He woke her a little before midnight and she quickly went to the bathroom; she'd learned to call it "the head" as Jared did for some unknown reason. She splashed water on her face and went on deck. The wind was still from the southwest but had strengthened a little. He had taken a nighttime reef in the main and seemed satisfied with the set of the sails. He settled down on the lee cockpit cushion and closed his eyes.

"Course is northeast, full and bye."

"Northeast, full and bye, aye Captain," she replied, and watched him fall asleep as quickly as she had a few hours before.

She watched the compass, making sure she stayed on course. To her this was akin to climbing a tall ladder and being told not to look down. She admitted to herself that she was scared; all she had to do was look down to see how tightly her own hands were clenching the wheel. She looked at the sails in the way he had taught her and then at the sea. But the sea was just blackness now, and it was running by *Chauffeuse* at an amazing rate. The strengthening waves were lifting her and dropping her in a regular rhythm. Then, every once in a while, the rhythm changed and she had to get accustomed to the new one.

And above it all was the huge night sky. Dee had never seen so many stars in her life. It looked like a giant web of jewels set on a black velvet background. *I am so small and insignificant; what do I matter in this huge universe?* She wanted to wake Jared to share her thoughts but then she looked at him resting peacefully and took a deep breath. *How could he sleep through this? Has he been sailing for so long that he takes all of this for granted? Does he ever wonder about our place in the universe?* Her mind kept working. *And he trusts me to stand watch from midnight until four a.m. while he sleeps.*

She straightened up and looked again at the dark sea and the sails and the stars and said out loud, "Damn it! I can do this!"

She relaxed her hands on the wheel and corrected the course slightly.

Jared seemed to smile in his sleep.

The next two days were idyllic. They talked about the gallery and what she hoped to do with it. She told him stories about her favorite clients and the artists she knew and hoped to find again. He told her about his youth and the start-up companies he'd helped over the years.

The sea was smooth and the wind was steady until late afternoon on the second day, when a line of storm clouds appeared on the horizon. The breeze kicked up and Jared knew from experience that the weather was going to change. Dee was below deck taking a nap, so he lowered the mizzen, took in the staysail, and reefed the main. He'd wake her if the weather worsened.

Dee awoke as the motion of the sailboat suddenly changed. While before the rolling motion was regular, now it seemed that *Chauffeuse* was pitching and fighting her way through the water. She struggled out of her bunk and started up the companionway. When she got to the top and looked out, she understood why— they were in a storm! She saw Jared and froze for a second; there was wind and rain in his face and his hands were holding tight to the wheel. But she could see that he was calm in the way that only a sailor could be when he knew he had control and full confidence in his boat to ride it out. She started to come out on deck. Suddenly she heard Jared shout, "No, get you gear and your life jacket on!"

He'd never yelled at her like that before—she wondered what she'd done wrong. She put on her foul weather gear and started back up on deck.

As soon as he saw her, she heard him shout again, "Dee, where's your harness? Get that on too!"

She realized he wasn't angry with her, but merely trying to protect her, and the only way he could do that was to shout over the wind and rain. She ran below and rummaged around until she found the harness. She had stuffed it away because she thought she'd never need it. *Who needs this? I'm not going to climb any mountains on a sailboat.* But she saw that Jared was wearing his and realized its purpose was to keep her from falling overboard and disappearing into the sea during storms like this one.

When she went back on deck, the storm hit her like a living thing. The rain lashed at her and the wind tore at her clothes. Jared motioned for her to come aft. She felt him bring *Chauffeuse* into the wind long enough for her to get down the weather deck to him. She worked her way along, bent over against the wind and not letting go of one hand-hold until she found another, not trusting herself to make a run for it. As she reached him, he grabbed her carabiner and snapped it onto the taffrail and then brought the boat back on course. She buried her face into his chest, feeling the strength of his shoulders constantly turning the wheel to keep them headed into the storm. The strength of his legs kept them both solidly balanced on the deck. Looking up, she realized she could hardly see the mainmast, much less the sea before them. He was steering by compass and relying on the feel of the sea and the way *Chauffeuse* reacted to it. He was in his element and she knew he wouldn't let her down. She lifted her head and looked into his face. He was enjoying this!

He looked down at her and she realized she'd forgotten her yellow Gloucester foul weather hat; her hair was plastered to her head. She stopped him from giving her his own rain hat, reaching up to kiss him instead. It caused him to fall off a compass point and brought a huge spray over the bow. After his hastily made correction, she snuggled back into his shoulder, content with the new course in her life.

———

Dee sat behind Jared most of the night until they sailed out of the storm. Finally, the wind and rain began to ease, although the seas were still churning. She'd been watching this man, the man she was so in love with, control the vessel and finally she shook her head.

Why didn't I find him sooner? And then, *where was I when he needed me?* She knew there were no answers to these questions. What was important was the present and the fact that they had found each other and had the future before them. She was pulled out of her reverie when he asked her if she would take the wheel for a little while.

"Now?" she asked. "In these seas?"

"I have great faith in you. Besides I need to answer nature's call. It's been a long night."

She laughed. "What's the course?"

"Zero three zero."

"Zero three zero," she repeated, as he disappeared down the companionway.

Dee couldn't believe how brave he was, given how scared she had been. She had no idea how his years of sailing had prepared him for storms just like this one. He was the most wonderful man in the world…in her world.

The storm was over now; dawn was breaking and the sky was that strange watercolor mix of pinks, blues, and grays. The few remaining clouds cast dark shadows on the blue water.

She smiled to herself. After all, he was a human being, in spite of seeming to be Popeye the Sailor Man. She laughed out loud at that and was still laughing when he came back on deck. "Do you like spinach?" she asked.

"No, why?"

"Never mind, just curious. Can I have more sail set?" she asked tentatively.

"Ask me properly."

"Permission to hoist the mains'l and shake out the reefs in the jib and mizzen! Sir!"

"Aye, mate," he said as he headed forward with a smile.

Dee smiled too and realized what she'd been doing; her bare feet seemed fastened to the deck but her legs had a mind of their own, balancing her in a dance with the waves. She saw the mains'l go up and sheeted home and, without thinking, corrected for the increased drive. It seemed that she too was now one with *Chauffeuse* and the waves. It was an exhilarating feeling she had never known before. *Like the world's biggest, longest roller-coaster ride.* She laughed and shouted out loud.

Jared watched her, knowing just what she was experiencing. He could see that Dee was beginning to understand his love for the sea; this trip had opened a whole new perspective on life for her. The storm had cost them time and brought them closer to shore than he'd wanted, so he decided to run into Charleston, South Carolina for rest and supplies. It would take most of the day to reach port, but it seemed like a good idea.

That evening, Dee observed Jared as he brought the large wooden ketch in under power through the still choppy inlet. He'd called ahead and had a berth waiting for them at the marina, so they could rest and relax for the night.

"What? Not sailing right up to the dock?" she asked.

"Nope," he said. "Wind and tide aren't right, and besides, I don't have to impress you this time. I did that once so you'd notice me."

"What?" she said again. "You did that to get my attention?"

"Yes, and it worked once, my love."

"And there I thought you were a beach bum in cutoffs delivering some rich guy's sailboat."

"Right again. Actually, I rented that particular berth in advance so I could get you to notice me."

"That was sneaky. I was sitting there trying to figure out how to seduce you!"

"I prefer the appellation 'calculating' or even 'problem solving' to 'sneaky.' Are you unhappy about how it turned out?"

She gave him a long, hard look that eventually softened. "Not in the least," she finally said.

"Then get the dock lines out," he ordered.

"Aye, aye, Captain," she said dutifully, although her eyes said something else.

In another few minutes their stormy adventure would be just a memory. Down below, the cabin was in disarray, and since they were both hungry, when Jared had called ahead for a berth at the marina, he had also ordered takeout from a local restaurant. "That was fair breath of wind last night, but you seem to have earned your sea boots."

"You old salt. I bet you just whistled up that wind to see if I could take it."

"Aye, and you did," he replied. "You're a sailor now, and *Chauffeuse* has a new first mate."

"You will never cease to amaze me," she said demurely with a contented smile.

Dock boys came to help them tie down for the night, and soon their catering order was delivered. Dee took their dinner below and spread it out on the galley table. As they shared it, with glasses of wine, they finally began to relax. The boat swayed gently at the dock and lulled them into a peaceful state. Jared thought about calling Melanie but decided it could wait until morning.

He finally took Dee by the hand and led her toward the master stateroom, removing his clothes as they went aft. He started the shower and tended to her, gently removing her shorts and top and testing the temperature of the water. It was a tight fit in the shower, but the water felt so good that she didn't care. She let it stream over her hair and face, while at the same time she held Jared around his waist, not wanting to let him go. He ran his fingers lightly down her face, then trailed them down the length of her torso, cupping her breasts and watching the water course over them. He pulled her close and kissed her; she felt his strength down the entire length of her body. She pulled him closer and invited him to bend down to kiss her again.

Drying off with soft towels, they fell into bed and were both asleep before they knew it. Sometime later, probably after midnight, they stirred and stretched. She heard his breathing change and she whispered in his ear, "Darling, are you awake?"

"Oh, yes, my sweet, and thinking wonderfully wicked things…"

She responded by stretching her body, catlike, and arching her back. He caught her around the middle and pulled her to him, gently lifting her on top of him. She settled there contentedly, and he began to use his hands and lips to awaken her body to his. This time it was long and leisurely and peaceful in a new kind of way. Their lovemaking became the journey, and suddenly they were in no hurry to reach orgasm and fall asleep. They were discovering how to pleasure each other almost completely…how to slow themselves and begin again after resting. She taught herself to listen for his breathing and to understand his body's signs. It was the most erotic lovemaking she had ever known, and she was so fully aroused that when they were both satisfied hours later, she fell into a dreamless sleep that lasted well into mid-morning.

Chapter 5

Aunt Em and Henry

WHEN IT CAME TO MATTERS of the heart, Auntie Em was about as sentimental as a woman could be. She loved Henry with a love that was both physical and emotional, and she treasured the memories they had made over the last twenty-five years. Her only regret was that although she was an aunt many times over, she had never become a mother. The men she'd met in her youth were passionate, but she did not consider them husband material, much less "father material." She had enjoyed many good times in her young years, both in and out of bed, but in none of these adventures did she encounter anything lasting.

Then, at the age of forty-five she'd found Henry. When she met him at a cocktail party for the opening of a new bookstore/ antique shop on Warren Street in Hudson, she knew he was a man of substance. Not necessarily of financial substance, but she saw immediately the potential for great passion and great conversation—her two loves and her two requirements for love. She saw depth and creativity and a sense of humor, all gently carved into a tall, good-looking man most beauties would pass over as not being quite showy enough. She was hooked! Henry looked down at the smiling woman with the ample bosom eagerly awaiting his next pronouncement, and he too was smitten. They were married six months later.

Emily smiled when she thought about the two and a half decades they had been together. They were wonderful years, full of adventures, with their latest, of course, having been the acquisition of a stately old mansion overlooking the Rip Van Winkle Bridge. They turned it back into an inn called Green Haven, which it had been in the 1800s; then they added a wing where the rooms looked authentic—as they must have looked at that time, but with cleverly camouflaged modern conveniences. Given the area's natural beauty, the comfortable accommodations, and the excellent care they gave their guests, it quickly became a success.

And the food! Em and Henry were both accomplished cooks and had even been mentioned in the *New York Times* culinary review section with a rating of 4.3 stars. They alternated between a six-burner gas top—also known as a piano among chefs—and a wood stove. Henry said that stew sitting on the back of the wood stove took on a flavor of its own and Em said that bread and muffins baked in the wood oven did the same. She got up early every morning to bake a fresh batch, and invariably, when the aroma filtered up the stairs, the guests would come down in their pajamas. It wasn't a pretty sight, but nobody cared. It was warm, comfortable, and relaxing.

The only reason the inn didn't have five stars was that one of the reviewers had been in a hurry and said the service was slow. "Learn to savor your food," Henry admonished him. "Enjoy it and the friends around you." Unfortunately, the lesson was lost on this particular individual.

But the ambiance that brought back repeat business was the common room. With the hand-hewn ceiling beams and the brick fireplace with a cast iron pot hanging on a crane, it was reminiscent of an inn from colonial times; it was the place for evening fireside chats. Comfortable couches and stuffed chairs with rustic wood tables made strangers into friends. Plus, there was the chess set—and no television.

Em could tell that Henry was getting on in years, given he

was seven—no, almost eight—years older than she. My goodness, she thought, he is rapidly approaching the age of eighty! It's no wonder his mind sometimes seems to be hunting for lost words, and he forgets he went out for wood and comes back with something else entirely. We shall have to talk about this sometime soon, she realized. Yes, we will have to talk about it...

She thought about the friends and colleagues they had made. She loved Jared like a son and was getting to know and like Dee very much, having become acquainted with her when she'd stayed with them before going to Las Vegas. She looked at the two of them—both in their thirties—and saw the same kind of love she and Henry shared. And then she thought wistfully that they could have children of their own and not just nieces and nephews. Em decided that Dee would make a wonderful mother.

It made her happy when Jared told her he was buying the land on Blue Hill Road and wanted to design a house that would be their own Hudson Valley retreat. Em knew the area and thought it was a beautiful place, and Jared was so pleased and proud to think about giving Dee this special present. He knew it would give her the roots she needed: roots that had been taken away from her as a child. She would have them back, and this time no one could take that away from her. She would be able to raise her children in that house.

Em also knew that Jared was knee-deep in another of his mysteries. In fact, the last time he'd had the group together at Green Haven, she had to keep shushing Henry so she could eavesdrop. Nowadays, it was all about computers and the trickery the young folks did with them. The Internet had done a lot of good for the world, but it was also a place where so much damage could be done because there was big money to be made by stealing from people. She knew about the romance scams, the bugs and the worms, and the phishing. Now she'd read that it was getting worse, and she was both horrified and intrigued. At times like this that she most felt the passage of time—watching the young people deal with the world's issues and feeling sidelined because of her age.

Stop it. She pulled an apple pie out of the oven and sighed. *You have it good, and you've had your fun.* Yet, she remained unconvinced. One more thing to talk to Henry about when they found a few peaceful moments. Maybe tonight, when the lights were out and all was quiet in the house. *Maybe pillow talk of a different sort tonight.*

Henry beat her to it. At dinner that night over the apple pie, he turned to her. "That was wonderful pie, Em."

She thanked him and then looked at him and waited. She knew there was something on his mind that he wanted to say, but he couldn't find the words.

Finally, he spoke. "You know that old shed behind the barn that I turned into my ham radio shop?" he asked hopefully.

"I do," said Em. "I do live here, remember? Before that you turned it into an illegal still to try to make whiskey, but no one would buy it because it tasted awful. And because they were your friends—if they bought it then you would get arrested and they didn't want that to happen. Now what in heaven is all that computer stuff doing out there?"

"Well, it's a long story, Em," he said. "I've been meaning to tell you about it, but I sort of have been sworn to secrecy. I told Melanie I'd have to let it all out. She said to go ahead, you probably already knew."

Jonathan eyed his father and said, "We had to get rid of Steve Milan, but what about that bimbo wife of his? I bet she knows enough to be a real problem for us. Maybe we could squeeze more about Steve's overseas contacts out of her. She could be really useful to us, or very dangerous."

Steve had run a shady import/export business, and his next big money-making deal was supposed to come from a new contact he was working with in Morocco. However, Jared and his Protek team brought him down before he was able to make contact in Las Vegas. There were a lot of unanswered questions since then, and a key item—a briefcase containing important information—was never found.

Jonathan had a very bad feeling that Dee either had it or knew how to get her hands on it. And that worried him—a lot!

"I am already well acquainted with Steve's Moroccan connection," replied Joseph. "Steve was already approaching the end of his useful life, and as I said 'When the golden goose starts laying rotten eggs, it's time to find another goose.' Do nothing to Dee because now she is loved by Jared Herreshoff. He loves her as I loved your mother. Remember when I was asked by Ahmed whether anything should be done about him, I told him, 'If you like petting cobras, be my guest.' He agreed. We don't need to cultivate enemies, Jonathan; we have more important business to consider and we don't need him or his security agency after us."

"But she could compromise us!" exclaimed Jonathan.

"Don't raise your voice to me," said his father, an icy calm in his voice. "The decision is mine and you will obey."

Jonathan was unhappy, but he nodded, still angry about being forced to witness Steve's execution. He was even angrier thinking that Dee might know things that could implicate him in his criminal activities. He decided to resolve the situation even if he had to disobey his father.

But first he had to find Dee.

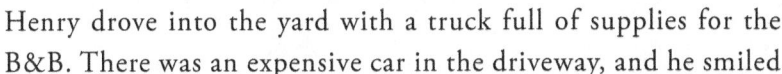

Henry drove into the yard with a truck full of supplies for the B&B. There was an expensive car in the driveway, and he smiled at the anticipated business. He decided to wait to unload and instead went inside, intending to surprise Em. He hefted a bottle of peach schnapps, their favorite, and headed for the back door.

Loud voices stopped him cold.

"Where the hell is Dee?" shouted a male voice.

Em's voice: "Go ahead, sonny, hit me! Would you do that to your own mother?"

Hearing Em's stressed voice galvanized Henry into action. He flipped the bottle so he was gripping the neck and charged into the room. Em was sitting in one of the kitchen chairs, both arms held behind her by one man. Another was about to slap her, but her shout stopped him cold.

Henry slammed the bottle of schnapps right on the point of the man's shoulder; the man screamed in pain as his left arm went useless. Henry followed with a blow to his nose; blood spurted, and the man was out of action. The first man let go of Em and reached for his gun. Seeing this, Em grabbed her rolling pin off the table and backhanded him in the face with it. Same thing Henry had done but the results were slightly different. He went over backward but still managed to fire a shot. Unfortunately, Henry got in the way of the bullet.

Actually, the bullet ricocheted off one of Em's favorite cast iron pans that was hanging on the wall, and it hit Henry on the rebound. He was more pissed off than wounded. He administered some heartfelt blows to the two men while Em rummaged around in the kitchen junk drawer looking for her Colt 45. She finally found it.

Henry collapsed into a chair.

"Are you hurt badly?" asked Em.

"Not bad, but I'm tired of this Kung Fu stuff."

"Here"—she handed him the gun— "see what you can do with that."

Henry looked at it and then at Em. "How many times do I

30

have to tell you that a single action needs to be cocked before it goes off?" he said ominously, pulling back the hammer.

"I know, I know," she said, rummaging around in the same drawer for their handcuffs, which she then used professionally on the two intruders. Then she read them their rights and finally called 911.

"Who the hell are you?" asked the one who had been about to slap her.

"We're both deputy sheriffs here in Columbia County, so you two have assaulted the police force and are now in deep, deep trouble. Now let's hear your names." The men were silent.

Henry was beginning to go into shock, so Em took the gun from him and found a dish towel to staunch his wound. "I'll be okay, Em," he said, as the sirens wailed outside.

In the emergency room, Em sat by Henry while the bullet was extracted and the wound was bandaged. The doctor told them that most of the bullet's power had been diminished by something in its trajectory and had finally been stopped by a rib in Henry's side.

"I've had worse dog bites," grumbled Henry.

"Well, my favorite cast iron pan is perfectly fine," said Em.

"Yeah, and if the bullet had been six inches to the left or right, it would have gone through the wall and I wouldn't be lying here," he grumbled again.

"You're a lucky man," said the doctor. "You've been shot before and survived, I see. The one in your chest must have been serious."

"Vietnam was the first," said Henry.

"He got a medal for that," said Em. "Took the bullet and kept fighting until they had to retreat and then carried another wounded soldier out of enemy territory."

"I don't want to go through that again," mused Henry. "The second was when some idiot from downstate thought deer wore orange jackets. Shot me in the ass! Hurt like hell. Stupid hunter was so surprised; he called all his friends over to see what he'd shot. I waited until they got close and then stood up, showed them my badge, and told them they were all under arrest. The hunter had made a rookie mistake and I didn't have a warrant, but they didn't know that. They spent an uncomfortable night in jail while I got my ass sewn up. We let them go right before their expensive New York City lawyer showed up to bail them out. Hope he charged them a bundle. They're banned from hunting in New York in perpetuity and the lawyer told me they should have been banned before they ever got their licenses."

The doctor left and Em pulled out her cell phone. "I think it's time we called Melanie."

"Yup, Em, it sure is."

Sandra, the chief at the desk in the Columbia County police station was a thirty-year veteran. She had borne and raised six children, all of them boys and two of them policemen. She could be pleasant and helpful when people came in with complaints about petty theft of chickens or to pay traffic citations. She was more stern with the repeat bar fighters every weekend. But at this moment, she was angry enough to stare down a Marine drill sergeant. She knew Em and Henry—they'd shared meals and potluck dinners. They were her friends.

"State your name," she asked the first man in a controlled tone. Silence greeted her interrogation.

"You are required to identify yourself." Again, no response.

"All right, I will enter that you refused to identify yourself. You should know that both of you will be charged with attempted first-degree murder of a police officer. There are more charges, but I'll let the local prosecutor enumerate them. I suggest you cooperate because your fingerprints are now being processed by the FBI. I'll bet this isn't your first rodeo," Sandra said with a thin smile that did not reach her eyes.

No response.

"All right, have it your way. But you are not going to get that call to the high-priced lawyer you want to retain until you STATE YOUR NAME!"

An "oh shit" look crossed his face, so he gave her his name—Jonathan Benefacio—his residence, and all the other pertinent data. She finally finished filling in all the requisite blanks, plus a few that didn't need to be filled in at all, just to keep him waiting.

"What's the other clown's name?" she asked, cordially.

"Tony," said Jonathan, without hesitating. As it later turned out, Tony wasn't his real name, but it gave Sandra a reason to fill out another complete set of forms.

"Can't you hurry up?" demanded Jonathan. "He's the one who pulled the trigger."

Sandra gave him a long, hard look. "I already knew that," she finally said. "But you hired him and brought him here, so you are as deeply implicated as he is in the premeditated, attempted first-degree murder of a police officer. Think about *that* while I process you."

She eventually handed him the phone. "Now you can make your call," she said.

"Don't I get some privacy?"

"Not in this corner of the county, you don't. You may have noticed we have only one cell, limited office space, and a minimal budget. Make your call now or not at all."

Jonathan reluctantly lifted the phone. Sandra memorized the number he punched in without a change of expression. After all, she could play poker with the best of them on Saturday night at Jake's bar if they'd let her. It depended on how much money she'd taken from them the previous weekend. She may have looked otherwise, but Sandra was no hick cop.

He finished his call and was led back to the cell to spend two uncomfortable nights and most of the next two days. Sandra was on the phone to Em with all the information and Melanie galvanized her staff. Even with Irving, Ellen, and Karen on the road, she had enough people to track all of this down.

At their home, an elegant brownstone in Boston, Mary Rose sat in the corner of the living room watching her brother. Her father, Giuseppe Benefacio—also known as Joseph Benefactor—looked at him without affection.

"Why did you let me rot in a stupid hick jail for two days?" Jonathan shouted. "You could have had me out in two hours!" He ranted on until his father waved his hand dismissively.

"Not from there," said his father calmly. "You don't know who you are playing with. I told you not to go looking for Dee, and you disobeyed me! Now Jared and his whole company are going to come down on us with both feet. I have a lot of politicians in my pocket, but he has the whole damn federal government in his. How can I make you understand, Jonathan?" He suddenly roared, shaking his fist at his son. "If Jared Herreshoff says he wants you to spend four years in prison with an inmate who hasn't seen a woman in ten years, there'd be nothing I could do about it. Now get out of here. Your arraignment is tomorrow."

Jonathan left. Mary Rose looked at her father with a raised eyebrow.

"I had such great hopes for him," her father said, "but he never understood what it took to be a leader. Now you are all I have left, Maria Rosa," he said, using her given name.

She curled her bare feet up under her on the chair and smiled at him.

Early next morning after the storm, Jared put in a call to Melanie. He'd asked her to limit her calls because he was on vacation for the first time in a long time. While she had acceded to his wishes, her patience was wearing thin and she was happy to hear his voice.

"Jared, I'm so glad you called. We have some problems here. Two men came looking for Dee at the B&B. When they didn't find her they tried to get Em and Henry to tell them where she was. But you know those two—they got the best of those young thugs pretty quickly. Seems they did some time in the Columbia county jail as Sandra's guests."

"Are they okay, Mel?"

"Henry took a bullet, but he's going to be fine. He's more angry than he is hurt. But they are both worried about Dee's safety. By the way, one of the thugs was Joseph's son, Jonathan."

There was a long pause and then Jared said in an overly calm voice, "I'll speak to Joseph."

Melanie gave an involuntary shudder.

"I trust Sandra showed them Columbia county hospitality," Jared said mirthlessly.

"Oh, yes, I'm sure they did *not* enjoy their stay—and I can't imagine why it took so long for their lawyer to get them released. Must have been some paperwork foul-up," she said sweetly.

"Thanks, Mel, I hear your hand in this. Dee and I are in Charleston. Could you send the corporate jet down to pick us up and take us to Washington? And do you think you could find my captain, Barney, and ask him to call me? I'd like him to assemble a crew and take *Chauffeuse* to a little dockyard in Norfolk, Virginia, that I've found. They specialize in wooden boats. I'll tell him what I want done if he thinks they can do it. Tell him I'd like him here as soon as possible."

"Jet to Charleston to bring you and Dee to Washington. Barney and crew to sail *Chauffeuse* to Norfolk. Anything else?"

"How's the baby doing?"

"Kicking up a storm. I think he's going to be a sailor."

Jared laughed for the first time. "Don't talk to me about storms! See you soon, Mel, and thanks."

"You're welcome, admiral." And then she hung up.

Later that morning, Jared brought Dee her first cup of coffee. She pulled herself up to a sitting position, trying unsuccessfully to rearrange the bedcovers. She could see that Jared had something on his mind. "Change of plans," he told her. "Just a slight change in plans. How quickly can you get your things into an overnight bag?"

Chapter 6

Washington, DC

THEIR JET TOUCHED DOWN AT Reagan International early in the afternoon, and they caught a cab to Jared's Watergate apartment. He had both their overnight bags slung over his shoulder, and he dropped them on the nearest chair inside the door. Dee's eyes were drawn to the windows, and she wandered toward them in a daze. "Oh my God, Jared, this view is incredible! I had no idea this is where you lived... how you lived."

"Happy that you like it, my darling," he said. "This has been my primary residence for a long time, and when we're in DC, this is where we'll stay. It seems like I'm always on the road, but with you in my life now, I'd like the two of us to spend more time here."

"Are you always on the road? Is it because you *have* to be or because you *want* to be?" She looked up at him with so many questions in her eyes. He stood behind her with his arms around her protectively. She leaned back into his arms, feeling his strength and his love surround her. "My darling," she said quietly, "I have never felt so loved, so cared for, as I have in these past few weeks. It's as though you know what to say, what to do, what I need, even before I do. It's uncanny."

"I think part of it is because I'm so in tune with you. But right now I'm at a loss. What would you like to do first? After all, we've been on the road (well, actually, on the boat and on a plane) for what seems like forever. Are you hungry, tired?"

She swayed in his arms as she admired the view from his living room. "Well, first of all, please give me the tour, and then let's shower and change and go in search of something to eat... and, oh, I think I'd enjoy—no, I think we'd enjoy—a little nap. Would you like to start by pointing me in the right direction?"

Jared did exactly that. And, as he showed her around the two-story penthouse, he thought she might like to add some of her own touches to the masculine décor he'd lived with for the past decade. He'd never brought a lady friend up here in all the years he'd owned it. Once in a while he would host a small dinner party for his Washington insiders, but then he would call a local restaurant and ask them to send up dinner, complete with a bartender and waiter. The only woman who'd ever spent any time around this place was the cleaning lady he'd had for years, and he wanted to introduce Dee to her sometime soon.

Suddenly he was looking at his home through Dee's eyes, wondering what she thought of the art, the color scheme...even the curtains, the dishes and the linens. He would want her to put her mark on it, of course, and wondered where she would start. This business of looking at the world through her eyes was totally new to him, and he was beginning to like the feeling. Yes, he thought, his life was certainly going to change with Dee in it. Then he remembered he needed to call Melanie.

"All set, Jared. Barney's on his way with a pickup guy named Joe Oxford. He says he tried to get onto your crew once before but didn't quite make it."

"I remember him. He'll do and maybe I'll give him another chance; its Barney's call. I'll wait for his opinion on the yard."

"Aye, aye, sir," said Melanie and Jared could feel her smile through the phone.

Meanwhile, Dee luxuriated in the large shower stall with the Amazon rainforest shower head. After the cramped shower stall on the boat, this felt heavenly. She found the fragrance of Jared's special soap and shampoo to her liking and was lathering her hair for the second time when he joined her.

"Oh, Jared, this is wonderful! I'll probably take two or three showers a day until I've had my fill. You don't mind, do you?" He didn't say a word, but showed his acceptance by hugging her under the streaming water until the large glass shower stall was engulfed in fragrant steam.

Hours later, after they'd gone for a walk, picked up some takeout dinner from the neighborhood Indian restaurant, and watched the evening news, Jared showed her his office. It was more like a command center than an office, however. There were monitors Jared could use to videoconference with his key people, as well as several computers and other pieces of equipment.

"Dee, I'm going to check in with Melanie now. Would you like to sit in?"

"Of course. Ever since I heard her voice I've wondered what she looked like."

In a minute Melanie was on screen with Jared. Even pregnant, it was obvious she was made of stainless steel and rawhide; she was all business. She acknowledged Dee quickly and then began to fill Jared in on all that had happened since their last conversation.

"Jared, we have several startling new developments." She emphasized the word startling, instantly raising Dee's level of attention. "Would you like that information *now*, or would you prefer to wait until the morning briefing?"

Dee looked at Jared, her eyes wide with fear.

"If there's bad news, or news about Steve, do you want to hear it now, Dee?"

"Of course," came her reply, and she refocused her attention in an instant.

Melanie began her report. "We now know this for certain, Jared, Dee, that Steve is no longer alive." Dee sucked in her breath and looked at Jared, who was stone-faced.

Melanie continued. "Our people had nothing to do with it. In fact, we did everything we could to get him back to New York in one piece, safe and sound, although in fact, a whole lot poorer than when he went. That part was planned. Our people watched him until he arrived back at his apartment, and at that point we ceased our surveillance. That turned out to be a grave error."

"What we did not know at the time was that he was taken away soon after he arrived home and that his end came shortly after. We have the information corroborated from someone who was at the scene of the crime and let it slip while talking to Em. We have no body, and most likely we'll never have one. We did consult with Bart to see how to handle Dee's future, and he verified that one of the documents Steve signed was a power of attorney over this legal action, which Bart executed, so Dee is now officially divorced. The remainder of his estate will not go to probate for seven years unless we can provide irrefutable evidence of his death. Not that he had much cash left. But he did own the New York apartment and one heavily mortgaged yacht."

Dee looked at Jared, stunned and speechless. She could see in his face he wished he'd waited until morning so he'd have had time to prepare her. Too late now, she thought.

She took it one step further, wondering how their plan to ruin Steve financially had escalated into his murder. She was horrified, but it also became clear as she ran Melanie's conversation through her head that Jared and his crew had ruined him financially, yes, but they had also stayed with him to protect him from harm.

Suddenly one thought was uppermost in her mind: someone else, someone powerful and ugly, had wanted Steve dead! A shiver of alarm and fear coursed through her body. What had seemed like a silly game in Las Vegas had turned deadly—and it was close to home—way too close for comfort.

———

Joseph Benefacio's cell phone rang with the ringtone from Mimi's death aria at the end of *La Boehme*. He liked it and often hummed it when he walked down the street.

He answered as he usually did. "Talk!" He did not expect to hear the voice that came on the line.

"I will be in Boston at your office at 10 a.m. tomorrow. We have some things to discuss." The line went dead. The benefactor shook his head and wondered how this man had discovered his private cell number. He pressed the button for his secretary and told her to have his son and daughter in his office at 9:30 the next morning.

Petting the cobra, he thought, would have to be stopped.

———

Jared and Joseph looked at each other for several moments before speaking. They were both shrewd judges of people. Jared's first thought was that Joseph looked like a hawk—a bird of prey with eyes as cold as ice. Jared knew Joseph had not survived as long as he had in this business by being benevolent. In that respect, thought Jared, he's as much of a businessman as I am…except that he'd had Dee's ex-husband wrapped in chains and thrown into the Hudson River and forced his own son to witness it.

———

Joseph, for his part, saw a young man who was larger than life. He knew Jared had made his fortune turning around struggling companies. Their paths had crossed before; he could think of at least three companies he'd wanted for himself that Jared had snatched away from him. He'd also heard how Jared stripped Steve of almost every penny in a sting operation—one he had to admire. In fact, that was why he'd dropped him in the river. Steve didn't have what it took to play in the big leagues.

Jared was tall, lean, and fit. You could tell by the way he moved that every muscle in his body was ready for anything. His face was tanned and handsome when he smiled, which it wasn't doing now. And the eyes—the eyes that were boring into him—were piercing. Joseph shuddered. He knew his son was incapable of taking Jared on; he wondered if he was, after all these years.

"I apologize for my son," Joseph finally said. "He is always late."

"In my business," said Jared, "if you are not there five minutes before the meeting begins, you are late."

"A good rule," said Joseph. "I shall remember it."

The door opened and Jonathan came quietly into the room, on alert the minute he saw Jared. He looked at his father and sneered. "What's he doing here?"

"We need to have a serious discussion about your behavior."

Jonathan slumped into a chair; his unfocused attitude was not lost on his father. They looked at each other: Joseph with disappointment.

"You realize he's going to jail for what he did to people I hold dear," said Jared.

"Mea culpa," said Joseph. "I warned him not to 'pet the cobra' but he ignored me."

Jared showed just the hint of a smile; he hadn't realized what a reputation he had.

"What do you suggest?" he asked.

"I don't want my son to go to jail. I'm asking you to have the charges dropped."

"One of my relatives had a bullet removed from his side—a bullet that ripped into him in the presence of your own son. Why should I not press charges?"

"I might have some information that would interest you."

"Go on."

"I know where Steve is."

Jared considered him for a moment. "That doesn't interest me. I know he's dead and I know Jonathan was there. The location of the body is of no matter."

Joseph's left eye twitched, something that didn't often happen to him. He looked at Jonathan, whose unfocused eyes flickered nervously from his father to Jared. Mary Rose watched with the smile of a feral cat about to make a kill.

"What do you want?" asked Joseph.

"Something I can use," said Jared.

"What would that be?"

"Information."

"About what?"

"I don't know yet. But when I need it, I will come to you."

Joseph recognized an obligation when he heard it.

"Yes," he said, "I understand." Then, as quickly as it began, the meeting was over.

Chapter 7

The Gathering at the B&B

THE SUN WAS ALREADY BEGINNING to set, and the trees in the median cast long shadows on the passing cars, as Ellen and Irving drove up the New York State Thruway in their rental car. They chatted as she drove and he worked on his laptop in the passenger seat.

Earlier that morning they had boarded a flight in Washington, DC, landing in Newark shortly before noon. Irving was still trying to annotate and digest all of the information that came out of their meeting with DJ. Before the meeting, he'd thought note-taking might spook the kid, but DJ had been so busy looking at Ellen's chest that he wouldn't have noticed if television cameras had been recording his every word.

"We should talk this over with Jared and Melanie before the general meeting, don't you think?" asked Irving.

"Of course, hon," answered Ellen, turning the headlights on to counter the rapidly fading daylight. "There are so many implications, I can't begin to get my mind around all of them. The kid has his fingers in so many pies..." her words trailed off.

"The damned Russian mafia," he grunted. "Well, I'm not sure they're Russian. They could be any nationality, for that matter. The kid calls them Russian, but who knows? Just because one of them is named Boris..."

She interjected, "Can we somehow classify the things DJ told us, maybe write down all the schemes he's involved in?"

Irving began, "Okay, there's the credit card scam thing.

Melanie will be interested in that. And the gambling business. That fits right in to our Las Vegas piece, although he didn't actually mention Vegas. I thought he might be diverting funds out of online gaming operations in Central America. There were other clients, too, but I think those were the two main ops."

"But what about what he calls the Robin Hood part? Is he in big trouble over that?"

"Of course," he said, "but they'll have to catch him first. I'll explain it all to Jared and Mel and ask if we can take him under our wing—so we can protect him—and use him all at the same time. DJ's only now beginning to realize he's in *way* over his head, and he came to us at the right time. Another week or two and it might have been too late."

She nodded and patted his knee protectively.

Hours later, after several cups of coffee in the living room at the B&B, Melanie came to the same conclusion Ellen and Irving had reached on the drive up from Newark.

"You're right on all counts, Ellen," said Melanie. "He's in way over his head and now he's in danger from sources whose identity is presently unknown to us. And he could be a valuable asset to us in identifying—and possibly bringing down—the criminal masterminds behind some major worldwide scamming operations."

Jared nodded agreement and looked over at Melanie, who sat uncomfortably in an oversized couch, shifting her weight in an effort to find a position that would alleviate her discomfort. Instead, she stood up, arched her back, and returned from the kitchen with a straight-back chair. Sitting down again, her first comment was, "I love my darling Mitch, but I didn't know what an aching back I'd have when I was carrying his baby boy around all day. Can't wait until this kid is born so I can hold him in my arms instead." She continued. "I think we shouldn't waste any time bringing DJ on board. I have lots of room for him down in Crystal City. Do you think he'll come?"

Ellen smiled in her direction. "We didn't exactly ask him that question, but I think we can spirit him out of there quickly enough. How soon can you set something up, Melanie?"

"Give me two or three days, okay? Like early next week. Get him out of his apartment, fly him down to DC and get him into a nearby hotel. Then I'll send my people up to New Jersey to pack his stuff, like his computers, and either bring down or duplicate anything you think he'll need. It'll take me a day to transfer his phone number, but in the meantime, if anyone calls we will patch the call through to wherever he's staying. Will that work?"

"I can be his contact," said Ellen quickly. "I'll call him and set it up. The only thing is, he's used to having lunch with his mother once a month—the first Sunday, if I remember correctly. We'll have to fly him to New Jersey for that. Other than that, they only talk on the phone."

"No problem," said Melanie. "I have empty space in the warehouse behind our offices. We'll try to make his new 'office' look as much like his old one as much as possible. Take lots of photos, okay?"

"Oh shit," said Ellen. "I almost forgot. The kid has three cats."

Melanie groaned, and added kitty litter to the kid's shopping list. She hoped he didn't have any more idiosyncrasies.

It was a chilly Sunday morning in early November, and the B&B was filled to overflowing. Jared's Protek Group "dream team" was gathered in the Hudson Valley, so his key staff people could meet face-to-face. It was a luxury they didn't often have, given how busy they all were at their far-flung jobs. Even though

Melanie was married to Mitch, his personal surveillance work often kept him far away from home. So she was happy to have him in her bed for three whole nights. She looked over at Ellen and Irving, who were enjoying the fireplace, and thought that for them it must be a pleasant change from their small apartment in Washington. Mark and Karen were there too. Karen had flown in from Las Vegas, where she had been setting up offices and living space for herself and for Ellen and Irving, who would be moving there after the holidays. Mark had been down in the Bahamas attending a hearing for Steve's goons, who were now sitting in jail, awaiting sentencing for the attempted kidnapping of Dee.

Melanie looked around and realized that Mark was the only single man among several happy couples. Technically, although Jared was still single, he wouldn't be for long. She was happy for him; after all, he'd introduced her to Mitch. She wondered how Mark's relationship with the petite Karen was going. Aunt Em and Henry were there too, not only in their capacity as hosts of the B&B, but also as valued members of Jared's team.

She thought that Jared and Dee looked especially cozy. She knew they were ensconced in "their room"—the largest suite, located at the front of the house, where they could relax, but Jared could also observe anyone entering or leaving the property.

The meetings and talks would last all day, but Melanie would also make sure there would be a little fun on the team's schedule.

Jared opened the meeting to review the projects that were underway or in the planning stages. First on the agenda was an update on the Las Vegas project, code name Whale Watchers.

"Update us, please, Karen, on plans for Project Whale Watchers," he said.

Looking elegant in black slacks and pink cashmere sweater

that accentuated her best features, Karen began with a joke. "Well, I guess you know that Vegas is in the middle of the desert, so the only whales we have to watch are the big spenders. And that is exactly what we'll be doing." A few appreciative chuckles came from her team.

"While some of our whales are legitimate, as you well know, not all of them are. Our mission will be to help the owners of the Bellagio identify the constant influx of new whales. The casinos spend huge sums of money on their VIPs, including comping penthouse suites and expenses and even sending private jets to pick them up. Now there are real whales, but we need to distinguish them from the phonies. It's not as easy as you may think because of the speed required to perform these investigations, which are worldwide in scope. Many of their new clients are coming in from Asia and the Middle East on short notice, so we need to perform these background checks thoroughly and quickly. And if they've been gambling in other areas of the world, we need to capture that data as well."

Ellen smiled knowingly at Irving. DJ's Cray super computer might just fill the bill.

By now Karen had everyone's attention, so she continued. "While the casinos spend a lot of money on their whales, they continue to be a profit center, because whales gamble huge sums of money—and, like everyone else, they do lose. The problem with the 'fake whales' is not only that they cost the casinos money on comps, they often come with schemes designed to win big, using a variety of illegal techniques, including counting schemes and others that we need to identify and clearly define. Our goal for Project Whale is twofold: one, determine the quickest and best process for our client to keep track of the 'real whales' and two, identify the fake ones—and their schemes—and keep them out of the casino…all without causing any bad publicity for the hotel or for Las Vegas."

While Karen was giving her presentation, Jared decided to return Barney's call. "What do you think of the boatyard?" he asked, after an opening discussion about *Chauffeuse's* condition.

"It has some really good shipwrights; a couple of them apprenticed at Mystic. They can repair any damage from your little excursion to Miami and back. It's mostly just varnish and polish. We could actually do it ourselves, but these guys are wooden boat fanatics. You should have seen their eyes light up when I sailed *Chauffeuse* in there. By the way, Joe Oxford is okay by me. He can hand, reef, and steer so I recommend we put him on reserve as trimmer or grinder for our next race."

"Good, let's do it. I'll have Melanie get in touch with you to make him an offer. Anything else?"

"Yeah, this yard won't be in business for long at the rate it's been going. This is a hands-on group and they're not watching their bottom line. In the first, place, they're not charging enough money for the materials they use and the kind of work they do. They also put in too many freebies just to make themselves happy. They're probably going to have to close in six, maybe eight months. That'll kill them and I hate to see a yard this good disappear. My recommendation, Skipper, is to buy them out as soon as possible. We could use a boatyard of our own."

"All right, I'll see what I can do. Thanks, Barney." Jared hung up. He understood what Barney had told him about the yard workers' passion for wooden boats. He grinned and called Melanie.

Karen smiled as a round of applause punctuated her presentation. "We were aiming for an immediate start, but Jared has just informed me that we might be waiting until after the New Year, as we anticipate the start of a heretofore unplanned project. But first, Mitch has a project he would like to tell us about. Mitch?"

Mitch gave Karen a big smile, and stood up. "Hi all, it's nice having us all together for a change, isn't it? Good to see you guys!"

"I guess you could call this a typical surveillance job," said Mitch. "The only not-so-typical part of it is, it's in Canada and it's gonna be in the dead of winter. On top of that, it's basically an outdoor job—so some hearty soul will need to pack his long johns." Laughter rippled through the audience, and someone remarked, "Sounds more like a punishment than a job." Mitch continued as though he hadn't heard, explaining the business end of the situation, and then quickly turned the floor over to Jared.

Jared walked up to the front of the room and invited Ellen and Irving to join him. From the moment he began to tell his audience what the two of them had just discovered in Newark, there was total silence. It was obvious this was something big. For now, Jared told his team, "We are calling this 'The Penny Scam,' and it will take precedence over all other projects until its successful completion."

Chapter 8

Letting off Steam

CROWDED INTO A BOOTH AT the local Irish pub, Karen, Mark, Ellen, and Irving tried to unwind before things got hectic again. Ellen had been pleased when Melanie suggested it. "The next few weeks are going to be crazy, so why don't you guys go out and have a few drinks? You know, blow off some steam. I can't drink, but there's no reason why you shouldn't."

"What a day it's been," exclaimed Ellen. "There's so much going on, and when you get everyone together you can really see how many projects we're working on." Three heads nodded in agreement. It was clear to Ellen that they were a little overwhelmed, still trying to take in all that was going on. She looked at her dear Irving, thinking how lucky she was to have this nerdy-looking man in her life. He was so good to her and such a wonderful lover. She sighed out loud, and as she did, so did Karen. They exchanged glances and laughed.

The guys continued to sip their drinks, quietly and thoughtfully. Ellen jokingly thought that their brains were still at work even though their bodies were in the bar.

At first, Ellen didn't see the man who drifted over to them, but then she noticed he was tall and lean in his Levis, even though he looked and acted a little out of place.

"Hi," he said, "the name's Walt. Would you like to dance?"

"Sorry," said Ellen, "we've got other things on our minds."

"How about you?" he asked Karen and then looked at Mark.

51

"I guess not," he said.

Not to be put off, he said amiably, "Anyone for a game of darts?"

They all shook their heads.

"Oh come on," he persisted. "Let's have some fun."

Ellen watched as Irving stood up. "You know, I think I need some time to consider what we've been thinking about. It wouldn't hurt me to take a break."

The other three just looked at him and shook their heads, hiding their smiles. Ellen knew about Irving, and no doubt so did her colleagues.

Walt didn't.

"Okay, Walt, what's the ante?"

"Ten dollars too steep for you?"

Irving put his money on the table.

Walt's first three darts went into the seven, nine, and eight rings.

Irving's were in the six, seven, and nine rings. He looked at the darts reflectively.

"Another round, double or nothing?" asked Walt.

Irving put fifty on the table. "Let's make it more interesting."

Walt's first three darts went into the seven, six, and eight rings.

Irving's were so closely grouped they looked like they were all in the ten ring. But one was slightly out in the nine. Walt went to check and pulled the darts out of the board. Irving picked up the money from the table and turned toward Ellen.

Walt came back, grabbed his shoulder and turned him around. "That was just shit luck," he said. "You can't do that again!"

"Oh, yes he can," said Ellen sweetly. "All night long."

Then, suddenly, to her surprise, Walt whipped out a throwing knife and stabbed it into the table.

"Listen, twerp, I said it's double or nothing again!"

Irving pulled the knife out of the table and looked at Walt, shaking his head. Still looking into Walt's eyes, he flicked it at the dart board. It landed right outside the ten ring, effectively stopping all conversation in the pub.

"Shit! You can't ever do that again!" burst out Walt.

Irving looked away.

Ellen said, "Put your money where your mouth is, jerk." She reached into her bra, first pulling out her cell phone and then a folded up one-hundred-dollar bill.

Walt did his own fumbling and came up with a wad of bills to cover the bet.

Irving went back to the board and pulled out the knife. He hefted it and went over to the table. He stuck it back where Walt had left it.

He looked Walt in the eye and smiled.

In one fluid motion, he pulled the knife from the table and sent it flying toward the dartboard. This time it centered in the ten ring.

There was a moment of silence and then cheers went up as Ellen scooped up the winnings. She counted Walt's wad of bills and yelled at him, "You're ten dollars short!"

And then the shit hit the fan.

"Bitch!" he said, and went after her.

Irving got between them and his bulk slowed Walt down.

Walt's friends, always ready for this sort of dustup, got up to swing at anyone who'd swing back.

Irving swung a wild fist at Walt's head, but being a foot shorter, he missed.

Walt swung a punch at Irving, but being a foot taller, it sailed over his head.

Irving tried to knee Walt in the groin, but again his lack of stature hindered him and instead he flipped over onto his back and landed on the floor. Walt tried to stomp on him, but Irving rolled under the table just in time.

The melee continued. The bartender picked up the phone, no doubt calling 911. Chief Sandra answered. "Again?"

"Yep."

"How bad?"

"Bring the shotgun—and an ambulance"

"On my way."

Karen was backed up against the bar and feeling safer now that Mark had thrown his body in front of hers. She watched him in amazement as he casually, quickly, and painfully reminded the remaining brawlers not to get too close.

Then things took a turn for the worse.

Walt kicked over the table and picked up Irving by the shirt to get a better shot at him.

It was all Irving needed. He head-butted Walt on the nose.

Walt let him drop as the blood began to spurt.

Irving changed his tactics and threw a punch at Walter's crotch but Walt blocked it.

Walt grabbed the knife from the dartboard and came after Irving.

Ellen screamed, pushed past Mark, and grabbed Irving, pulling him out of the way.

That left Karen in front of Walt with the knife coming straight at her.

Later she said she'd never seen anyone move so fast. Mark recovered his balance and used his right hand to grab Walt's wrist, sweeping it palm up. Mark's left came up into the back of Walt's elbow. Hard.

The sound of Walt's arm breaking brought everything to a halt. Walt moaned and the sound of sirens echoed in the background. People started to melt away; the locals left cash, as did most of the others, and the ones who didn't likely had their bills paid by those left on the floor.

Ellen, Karen, Irving, and Mark slipped out of the bar just before the police arrived. Huddled around the front table of the coffee shop across the street, they watched the cleanup operation at the bar. Karen asked Irving how he learned to throw darts and knives.

"I've always had great hand-eye coordination, even though I'm not built like Mark."

They all laughed. Mark looked like Michelangelo's statue of David and Irving's body looked like a butternut squash perched on toothpicks—with a large head and not much hair and a large, bulbous nose, but he did have twenty-twenty vision.

Ellen cuddled her hero. "I love you so much, my darling," she cooed.

Everyone laughed again.

Karen said thoughtfully, "Melanie told me to find out how you shuffle cards. I haven't a clue. Do you know what she meant?"

Irving produced the cards and showed her the trick. He swore them all to secrecy before he told her how it was done. That brought another laugh.

Mark was still holding Karen tight and she liked the feeling. He had probably saved her life a few minutes earlier. She hoped that protecting her had become more than just a job to him.

Chapter 9

Dee Goes Shopping

UPSTATE NEW YORK WAS A place Dee lovingly called "apple country," and she was enjoying the gorgeous autumn weather. While she wanted to dance in the orchards, she decided to go shopping instead. She wanted to buy something special for Jared—a ship in a bottle— and knew Hudson was famous for its antiques. After several disappointments, she found a shop where an elderly lady gave her the name of a man who made them as a hobby. "He's an old curmudgeon, but he might sell you one if you're nice to him; otherwise, he's not worth the time of day," the saleslady said. Dee thanked her and went on her way.

Mitch and Mark took turns tailing her, making sure she didn't see them. It was good practice. They noticed two other men trailing her. Mark caught up to Mitch. "Aren't those two the Amish guys we took out at the B&B last month?"

"Yup, here we go again."

Hans, accompanied by Georg, had Dee in his sights. He was still angry from their first attempt to kidnap her a month ago; it had gone wrong from the start. At first, it seemed like an easy job: overcome the old couple, grab the girl, and get out. He hadn't reckoned on Mitch and Mark being there to guard her and, even worse, he'd underestimated Aunt Em and Henry. He couldn't figure out how he and Georg ended up handcuffed to a steam radiator by a couple of geezers—and then been dragged off to court. When Jonathan finally bailed them out, his instructions were clear: "Don't fuck up this time. Get her!"

"This is going to be easy," said Hans.

"That's what you said the last time," said Georg. But then Dee turned down a secluded alley. "Gruss Gott. Mach' schnell!" It came out as a stage whisper in German. They moved quickly and silently after her.

———

As Dee turned into the lane where the curmudgeon had his shop, she had the feeling she was being followed. It didn't take her long to find out how right she was. Two men grabbed her by the arms; one held her right arm and the other her left.

"We work for a man who has some important questions to ask you," one of them said. "There are things he wants to know and if you don't answer, it will be very unpleasant for you. Some unhappy times we had to endure, that you caused us," he said, lapsing into German grammar.

Dee spat in his eye, just as Melanie had taught her, which surprised him. He let go of her arm—his big mistake. She slammed the heel of her hand into his nose and he howled in agony. He leaned back and raised his right arm to slap her across the face, but his hand wouldn't move—something immoveable was holding it. He turned, and there was Mitch, who hit him with a hatchet-like blow under the ribs. Mitch removed his gun, ejected the clip, and then racked the round out of the chamber as the man lapsed into unconsciousness.

Dee was still in the other man's clutches, but that didn't last long. She waited until his attention was diverted to Mitch's attack on the first man and then cleverly caught him off balance, driving her fist into his kidney, stopping him cold. Then she backed up to balance herself and brought her knee up between his legs. He dropped like a rock. She reached down and pulled out his gun and cleared it. Mitch smiled. Next, she bent down and pulled out the first man's sleeve knife and offhandedly threw it into the nearest door lintel.

"Where the hell did you learn that?" asked Mark

"Irving taught me. He's an amazing teacher; he can make you see the target deep in your mind and then follow it when you throw. It's a ninja thing," she said. "Melanie has had Ellen, Karen, and me on a crash course in self-defense. After she has her baby, we're going to work out together—all of us," said Dee, benignly. "The same kind of workouts you guys do."

Mitch and Mark just looked at each other.

———————

Em arrived on the scene with Henry, the local constable, having been called by Mitch. Mark waved good-bye as they drove up in their Ford F150.

"Hmmm, don't we know these two?" Em asked, a chuckle in her voice as she recalled the last time they'd encountered the pair.

"I believe so," said Henry. "Got your handcuffs?"

"Same ones as last time," replied Em.

Hans was beginning to come around but Georg was still in a fetal position, clutching his testicles. Neither was going to pose a problem for Em or Henry.

"What do you think, Em?" asked Henry. "Back to the last time when we handcuffed them to the steam radiator?"

"Well, I suppose if we hurry we could get these miscreants to the courthouse in time to get their paperwork done, so's they could be properly incarcerated, but I'm not feeling charitable at this time of day. Perhaps another night handcuffed to the radiator would do them some good? And it's getting a little cool this time of year in upstate New York, so maybe we should turn up the steam heat. What do you say?" she asked.

"Well, it seems reasonable, but I'm more than willing to provide all of the steam heat you're going to need tonight," said Henry, dumping them in the back of the truck.

Hans and Georg spent an uncomfortable night chained to the steam radiator in the kitchen of the B&B. The next day Em and Henry drove Hans and Georg to the station in the bed of their pickup, but not before they had an informative discussion about the previous afternoon's events. The boys had been reticent at first, but when Henry turned up the steam heat and he and Em sat down to breakfast, their resolve weakened. "Same scheissekopf as last time," Hans finally snarled.

It was enough.

"Not again," said Sandra, when she looked into the back of the pickup. "What is it this time?"

"They attempted to kidnap Dee," said Em.

Sandra took a long look at the men. "You jumped to the top of my unhappy list," she said quietly. "Give me a few minutes to talk to them." When she came back, she handed Em and Henry their handcuffs.

"Nice job subduing them. They're not bad hurt, maybe just enough to be painful. Hope it will teach them some manners. They confirmed Jonathan hired them to kidnap Dee. I'll keep them here for a while until Judge Carson gets back from his hunting trip. A little early before the season, but he likes to be out of the woods before the assholes from downstate arrive."

"I know how he feels," said Henry, rubbing his butt. "By the way, Em and I did have some help with these guys. They were pretty well subdued when we got there."

"Know who did it?"

"Yep."

"Gonna tell me?"

"Nope."

"Okay, get whoever-it-is to press charges by Wednesday and we'll go from there."

"Copy that, Chief."

Sandra laughed, "These guys may be bad, and they are going to have a tough second time here in upstate New York, but they still didn't make it all the way to the top of my unhappy list. I've got deadbeat dads who make my blood boil this time of year. Think your friends could help me find them?"

Em spoke up, "Henry's learned a lot about computers, what with the Internet and all, and I wouldn't be surprised. Just give him some names."

Appearing to give it some thought, Sandra wrote just one name down on a piece of paper and handed it to Henry.

"Wife and child abuse, four kids, forty-eight thou in back support and more in alimony. Find the bastard for me and I'll nail his balls to your barn door."

As soon as they returned home, Henry connected with Irving online. It took Irving just over an hour to get back to him.

"Sorry it took so long," he said, "but the mutt was using an alias."

"No problem," said Henry, joking. "I had to milk the cows anyway." Of course there were no cows at the B&B.

"Okay, here's the data. It's a ninety-eight percent match so it's pretty sure to be your guy. His record of misdemeanors matches, and it looks like he's moved on to bigger and better felonies, but no convictions. I'll email you the information. The bum lives in Poughkeepsie. Don't do it yourselves; send in the troops—he's a mean bastard," Irving said.

"Thanks, Irving," Henry replied. As soon as the email came

through he forwarded it to Sandra with the message, "Is this the clown you're looking for?"

Sandra called Em and Henry right back. Her surprised voice came through the speaker phone. "Yes, that's him! How did you do it?"

"I have my ways," said Henry, twirling the ends of the mustache he didn't have and winking at Em.

As soon as she got the email, Sandra called Frank, the chief in Poughkeepsie. They had met several times in Albany during conferences. He was six foot three, 230 pounds going on 235, in his early fifties, and twice divorced because he was a serious cop. She was almost six foot, 190 pounds and holding, in her early fifties, and widowed. They were a good match, although she'd never gotten anything more than a professional smile from him.

Sandra could hear the surprise in his voice. "Hi Frank, you've got a boy down there I want to talk to."

"Oh?"

She gave him the details.

"Well, I've bounced him up and down a couple of times but couldn't find anything that would stick."

"How does deadbeat dad sound?"

"I love it. Send me the warrant."

"Check your inbox."

"Is it legal?"

"The judge is out hunting and I'm deputized in his place."

"Good enough for me," he said.

Six hours later Sandra took the chief's return call. "Sandra, do you know what you just did?"

She listened, pleased to hear from him so soon.

"We've been trying to bust this drug ring for two years, but they always seemed to have advance warning about when we were coming. This time I hit them before they could move. Sad to say, it was one of my own deputies who was in on it. He's on the other side of the bars now. The man you named fired shots at us and was wounded by return fire. He'll recover to face charges. We're trying to figure out the street value of all the stuff we confiscated. There was a lot of cash—more than enough to cover the deadbeat dad debt. Although she can put a lien on it, it's state's evidence and can't be released until the trial."

"So when do I get him back up here to talk to him face-to-face?" she asked calmly.

"As soon as he's arraigned, I will personally bring him up to talk to you."

"Thank you," she said.

"Sandra," he said, "when I come up, will you have dinner with me?"

She was silent for a moment.

"I thought you'd never ask, Frank."

Later, Sandra called Henry, who told Em, who called Melanie, who was confused because she hadn't been in the loop, but eventually figured out it must have been Irving and called him on his cellphone to get the backstory. While the deadbeat dad ultimately confessed, just three days after his arrest, Sandra and Frank delivered a check for $50,000 from Protek to the mother and escorted her to the bank to deposit it.

Case closed, thought Sandra happily.

Chapter 10

Dee Lands in New York

J ARED WASN'T TAKING ANY MORE chances with Dee's life and safety. After her near-abduction, he called Melanie, asking her to have his pilot file a flight plan from Columbia County Airport to New York City, and warm up the engines – they'd be there in 30 minutes.

They touched down at 7 p.m. Since Jared hadn't been with her when the kidnapping attempt went down, he was more than a little bit shaken. "Our luggage will be sent here from the B&B tomorrow morning," he said. "I needed you out of there instantly, if not sooner. If someone wants you badly enough to try to snatch you in broad daylight in the middle of a crowded shopping district, there's no telling what they will do next."

"Now what?" Dee asked.

"Let's get to where we're going, and then we can talk, okay?"

The New York City cabbie left them off at a brownstone on the Upper West Side; Jared led Dee up the stairs, opening the triple-locked door into a quaint, little apartment.

"Jared, this place is perfection."

"Thanks, my darling, but I can't take credit for it. It's my mother's, although she doesn't come here anymore. She and my dad bought it years ago when it was the height of fashion to come into the city for dinner and a Broadway show. Now it sits empty, but if you'd like to use it I can get it ready for you."

"It looks like the perfect place for an art dealer to live," came her soft reply.

She was already climbing the narrow circular stairs to the bedroom loft that held a double bed and a small dresser. The main floor housed the living room, with its tall bay window with the cushioned seat, the fireplace, and the fifteen-foot-high wall of books and decorator items surrounding it. Valuable oriental carpets covered the floor of the living room, which was furnished simply with a velvet loveseat and two chairs.

"Jared, this place is magnificent, but so tiny!" said Dee. "How big? Maybe five hundred square feet?"

"Four hundred sixty-five, to be exact," said Jared. He was downstairs near the entry, checking the locks and the phone and turning on the water. "This level contains the galley kitchen and the only bathroom, but we can make do for a few days while I figure out what's going on. In the morning, when we make our coffee run, we can stop at the drugstore to pick up a few necessities. For tonight, we'll order in from the takeout menus in the kitchen drawer."

"And tomorrow morning can we call your lawyer and find out about the art gallery, too?" she asked.

"Of course," he said. "But first we need to make sure you're safe. Four hours ago you were nearly kidnapped. You are my first—no, my only—priority right now."

She joined him in the living room and snuggled close to him.

"I know. It was scary, and it all happened so quickly! I'm a little shaken, but once I'm with you, I feel safe."

"Well, this time," he replied, "I'm nervous too. I can't shake the feeling I'm dealing with more than criminal anger this time. I'm thinking we're dealing with *crazy* or drugged or some facet that is simply *not* rational. That's what has me spooked."

Jared's phone rang; it was Mitch. "First, I have to tell you that Dee was amazing. You don't want to get into a fight with her, boss. What she did to those two was incredible."

Jared looked at Dee and high-fived her. "Yeah, I hear she's

been working out on Melanie's training course. You might want to take your own advice."

"Anyway," continued Mitch, "Em and Henry took our boys home with them, instead of removing them to the county jail. I think they wanted to get up close and personal with them and get to the bottom of this little mess. They said Jonathan was in on it, but what was their plan? Bring Dee to Jonathan, question her, and then release her? I doubt it. Dee continues to be in danger, so keep her out of sight until we can locate Jonathan and put a watch on him."

Jared answered, "Okay, will do. Stay on this and let me know what you find out."

"Copy that. Take it easy, and give our best to Dee. She's one hell of a woman."

"That she is, Mitch. Thanks to both of you, buddy."

Jared ended the call and engulfed Dee in a huge hug.

"My God, Dee," he sighed, "I assumed it was all over when we left Las Vegas." He stared at her intently. "I thought Steve was going to kill you—drown you in the ocean and collect the insurance money. Then we rescued you from that. We even recovered the money he was trying to cheat you out of. And now Steve can't hurt you anymore. But I was too quick in making the grand assumption I'd saved you. So what's going on now? What does Jonathan want with you? When does this end? *How* does it end?"

Uncharacteristically, Jared went to the tiny bar in the sideboard and selected a bottle of aged brandy, poured a generous amount into each of two Baccarat crystal snifters, and handed one to Dee.

"This is not a toast, by any means. You are safe for the moment, but there won't be any *real* toast until I'm sure no one—and I mean *no one* on this earth—not Steve, not Jonathan, or anyone else related to them, will ever harm you or be able to hurt you ever again. Only then will I be able to really propose a toast to our future."

He sat down on the loveseat and pulled Dee down on top of him. He drew her close and kissed her. But this was a new kind of kiss, full of hunger, not romance. It was Jared at his most vulnerable. He needed Dee. He didn't merely think she was beautiful or that they would have a wonderful life together. It was a need so deep and so desperate that he clung to her as though he was afraid they were both surely drowning. And, then, as if she weighed nothing, he picked her up and carried her over to the tiny staircase leading to the loft bedroom. He felt her soft kiss on his neck, and then he watched as she slowly climbed the curving, narrow stairway, certain their lovemaking would be the most passionate they had yet experienced.

Hours later, they slept. Dee was curled up against his back, sleeping heavily and undisturbed. Jared was not as lucky, and sleep didn't come until nearly dawn.

Not in his wildest dreams, however, could he have imagined what the future held.

Across the street, a homeless person pushing a shopping cart settled down for the night, a sophisticated cell phone tucked into the sleeve of his tattered jacket. Only his eyes gave him away; he was on high alert and ready to eliminate any potential danger to Dee and Jared.

Chapter 11

From Bad to Worse in Boston

J ARED TRIED TO CALL JOSEPH, but his old cell number was
no longer in operation. So he called Irving, who was out
shopping but transferred him to Ellen, who came back to
him in four minutes and thirty-three seconds with Joseph's new
cell number.

"Thanks," Jared said.

"No problem, chief," she answered sweetly, "It's been a busy
day here."

Joseph was angry when his new cellphone buzzed. He had been
assured that no one would know this number unless he gave it to
them, and he hadn't given it to anyone. He picked it up.

"Talk!" he barked.

"Your son tried to kidnap Dee again," said a soft voice that
he recognized, along with the implications that went with that
simple sentence. Then the line went dead.

"Someone bring Jonathan to me," he hissed.

"Did I not instruct you to leave Dee alone?" Joseph shouted
at his son when he finally appeared. "Your idiotic actions have
jeopardized our entire business. Jared is now going to move
heaven and earth to get you convicted. We're going to be audited
until we won't be able make change for a twenty-dollar bill. He
will find out exactly what kind of work Steve did for us and

probably try to indict me too. Everything I've worked for all these years is going down the toilet!"

He paused to draw a breath. "Look at you. Already drugged at this time of day. I'm sending you to rehab to lose the damn habit. Your sister's going to run the business; she's much smarter than you anyway, with her big business degree. And when you get out, if you don't get sent to jail, you're going to work for her."

"But I thought it would be better to find out what Dee knows about Steve's business with us," Jonathan whined. "And if she knew I was there when we dropped him in the river."

Joseph shook his head. "And how did you expect to find that out? By asking her if she knew you were there when Steve was dumped in the river? Why don't you just tell her you did it? The result is the same. Then she'll know for sure and you'll have to drop her in the river too. You might as well tell her Steve worked for us. Mama Mia! How could you be so stupid? I had such great hopes for you," he said. "Best schools, anything you wanted, and look what you've done. You think I'm going to let you run the family? You couldn't lead an eight-year-old to the bathroom. Now get out of here. I've got calls to make to see if I can control this mess you got us into."

But first he opened his private fire safe that only he and his lawyer knew the combination to. He took out two documents, both labeled "Last Will and Testament" and looked at them sadly. One left everything to his daughter, the other to his son. That was the one he shredded.

Two hours later he called Jared and invited him to dinner.

"I would like to talk to you."

"Where and when?

"Mama's Trattoria on Hanover Street in North Boston, if it's convenient—eight tonight."

"I'll be there," said Jared.

When he came out of his father's office, Jonathan ran straight into his sister. He gave her a venomous look and proceeded to tell her what had been said. "You win," he said, thinking he'd deal with the little bitch when the dust settled.

"Do you think I like the idea of running this damn business all by myself? When Father retires, we'll divvy it up."

Jonathan thought for a moment. "He's never going to retire; he'll die first. And he won't let me run any part of it anyway. He's probably going to write me out of his will."

"Better get going," she said, smiling sweetly. "He hasn't had time to do it yet."

The lights went on in Jonathan's brain, even if they were dim bulbs. He could get rid of his father and Jared in one swoop and then scoop up Dee. It seemed like the perfect plan. The fact that they might have bodyguards or that he would need an alibi didn't enter his anger- and drug-soaked brain.

Later that day, as Mary Rose stopped by to chat with her father's secretary, she casually asked if she could have dinner with him that night. The secretary said she'd made reservations for him at Mama's Trattoria on Hanover Street in North Boston, at eight sharp. "An important meeting," she added gratuitously.

Mary Rose stopped by Jonathan's office to tell him when and where he could find them. With all this in place she sat back, smiled, and waited.

Jared and Mark pulled up in a limo in front of the restaurant. Although there was a "Closed" sign on the door, it was opened for them immediately. Jared asked Mark to stay outside and was escorted by the maître d' to a back booth. Two glasses of Chianti sat waiting. Jared looked at the bottle and smiled: Ruffino,

Riserva Ducalle Oro: not what you'd bring to a Wednesday Prince Spaghetti night in Massachusetts. The dining room's interior was paneled in dark wood and gave the impression of a well-used establishment that had seen many patrons come and go over the years. Jared imagined what the food would be like and decided he would like to come back and try it some other time.

A few minutes later a second limo arrived, and the bodyguard, Dominic, helped Joseph from the limo and they walked up to the front door of the restaurant.

"Do you two know each other?" Joseph asked.

Dom and Mark shook their heads.

"Mark, meet Dominic, Dominic meet Mark."

Dom read Joseph's gesture and led Mark to a table out of earshot in a corner where they had a good field of vision around Joseph and Jared, but were not noticeable unless you were looking for them. Dom could tell that Mark wasn't any happier than he was. They were of the same size and build, both fit and ready for a fight. He would love to have a go at his opponent, but he was professional enough to know that his primary job was protection.

Dominic reached into his coat pocket and immediately felt a pistol barrel pressed against his ribs. He was surprised at how fast Mark's reactions were. He placed his gun on the table and looked at Mark. After a long moment, Mark placed his own gun next to his.

"Someday," said Dom.

"Not tonight," said Mark.

And they settled down to watch and wait.

Joseph looked at Jared and apologized for being late.

"Traffic," he said.

"This is Boston." Both men smiled wanly and looked at each other for what seemed like a long time.

Joseph sat back and saw a man in the prime of his life, now with the love of his life and the years stretching before him. He thought about his own life with the woman he'd loved who gave him a son and a daughter. But then he thought about what he had to do to make this happen. The men he ruined, and yes, the ones he had to have killed, including Dee's husband. And now he needed to deal with his son and apologize to the man sitting across from him, looking steadfastly into his eyes. He closed his eyes and shook his head. He picked up the glass of Chianti, looked at it reflectively, and put it down.

"Blood," he said simply. "Too much blood."

Suddenly Jonathan appeared in the doorway and headed straight for his father's table. Dominic saw him first. "What the *fuck* is he doing here?"

Then Joseph saw him in the mirror and was halfway out of his chair when Jonathan pulled a nine millimeter pistol from his pocket and aimed it at his father.

Mark yelled, "Gun!"

The room exploded into action. The unexpected shout caused Jonathan to hesitate by a millisecond. By then Mark had his gun off the table and was bringing it down, when Jared was suddenly there. He hit Jonathan once in the stomach and took the gun away as easily as if Jonathan had given it to him. Now that same gun was aimed at Joseph. Dom brought his gun down to bear on Jared and then felt the muzzle of Mark's gun at his own temple. There was a moment of tense silence and then Jared set the safety on the gun in his hand and laid it on the table. Mark pointed his gun at the ceiling. Dom relaxed and pointed his at the ceiling too.

Joseph sat down shakily and looked first at the gun and then at Jared. "He was going to kill me," he said. "Wasn't he going to kill me?"

"Digitalis?" asked Jared.

Joseph fumbled in his inside coat pocket; Jared reached in and retrieved the vial, shaking out two pills. He gave them to Joseph, who quickly downed them with the Chianti.

Jonathan, still hazy but somewhat recovered, appeared determined to do what he came for. When Jared's back was turned, he grabbed his gun off the table and pointed it at his father's head. "Fuck you, old man," he said, and pulled the trigger.

The gun didn't go off; the safety was on.

Dominic and Mark brought their guns down automatically and simultaneously shot Jonathan, whose eyes opened wide in disbelief. Joseph stared back at him, pain filling his heart as he watched his only son slowly collapse to the floor. Joseph looked at the gun in Jonathan's hand and watched the life drain out of him.

He looked up at Jared. "I should kill you," he said, "but it won't bring my son back." There were the beginnings of tears in his eyes.

"You were right," said Jared, sitting back down, "too much blood."

Jared knew there was no consolation he could give Joseph; that might come later, so he signaled to Mark to put his gun away. Dominic did the same. It was over.

Mark carefully reached into his breast pocket, pulled out his card, and gave it to Dominic after they joined Jared and Joseph at the table. Sirens could be heard in the distance. It was going to be a long night.

Jared was quick to get on the phone to Dee, Mitch, and Melanie to tell them what had happened and to let them know they were all okay—before the TV stations got hold of the story. He finished his calls well ahead of the 11 p.m. news.

The local papers noted the killing of a small-time hood at a popular north-end Italian eatery. No mention was made of Joseph's heartache nor the sister's change in status to only child and sole inheritor of the family business. It did not go unnoticed at the local TV stations and newspapers that pressure had been brought to bear to keep things low-key.

The autopsy showed that Jonathan had suffered two bullet wounds—both to the heart and both fatal. The bullets were nestled less than an inch apart. Mark and Dom's guns were confiscated as evidence, and although they were held on personal recognizance for the death, they were eventually discharged for having done their duty as bodyguards in preventing the murder of their principals.

Steve's body was recovered from the Hudson River and the case was closed.

———————

Mark's cell phone rang on Monday morning, back in Washington, DC.

"Yes?" he answered.

"Need a workout?" came down the line.

Mark smiled. "Yeah, I've been getting soft lately, nobody to beat on. Where are you?"

"Here. In DC. In your reception area. You gave me your business card, remember?"

Mark laughed. "Put me on to Mickey; she'll let you into the gym and show you where to change. And then she'll call the ambulance when I'm done with you."

"Yeah, but it'll be your body in the bag, asshole."

"Looking forward to it."

Mark and Dom looked at each other across the ring. Neither wore any protective gear or gloves. Mark had no fear of Dom; he thought he was invincible and immortal and would emerge victorious. The first blows shook them both. They sank down deeper on their knees and went with the kicks, blocked and came back with the fists. Blood began to flow, but this time Mark ignored the pain and scored a major blow to Dom's stomach. Dom folded to the floor, but was by no means out; he swept Mark's legs and kicked him in the back.

"Stop it!" roared a voice. "Right now!" Both gasping for breath, Dom looked at Mark.

"Who the hell is she?"

"That's Melanie."

"Melanie—Melanie who?"

Mark smiled and put his hand on Dom's shoulder. "If I'm not mistaken, she's your new boss."

"Are you with us or not?" asked Melanie.

Dom looked at Mark again.

"I know you're not working for Joseph anymore and I can understand why. He's shutting down and doesn't want any old talent around. Mark and I expected you to show up. He wanted to go a few rounds with you to see how good you were. Mark?"

"Almost as good as it gets. He needs some training in the social graces, though…"

Dom punched Mark's bicep.

"You know, Melanie," he said, "The mosquitos are getting annoying this time of year."

"Enough," said Melanie. "I don't have time for your testosterone party. Dom, do you want a job or not?"

Mark watched the interchange as Dom looked at him and then back at Melanie. He knew instantly that Dom recognized Melanie as the boss.

"Yes," he said half under his breath, "and...uh, thank you, Miss Melanie."

"Good! Go see Mickey and she'll read you your rights. Training starts tomorrow morning. You have some skills that need work. See you then."

Dom looked at Mark, "Don't I even get time to bleed?"

"Not here you don't. See you in the morning."

Chapter 12

DJ Moves to Washington

MELANIE HAD SET UP PROTEK's headquarters in a nondescript, one-story building near Four Mile Run Drive in Arlington, Virginia. Jared's instructions were to equip it for maximum efficiency. While the outside looked like a warehouse, the inside reflected Melanie's drive for perfection. There was her own office, and behind that, Jared's well-appointed suite and conference room, visitors' offices for a dozen people, a state-of-the-art communications center, kitchen, and supply and copy rooms. Beyond that lay a large workout room and a two-lane lap pool, as well as a cavernous warehouse containing every imaginable type of vehicle and a maintenance center. Melanie considered her fleet to be of the utmost importance in recon work; the limos, trucks, jeeps, motorcycles, and even an ambulance were carefully maintained and ready to roll at a moment's notice. She even had a company that owned a large number of tractor trailer rigs on retainer to provide her with the ability to move large loads anywhere in North America.

She called them now to organize DJ's move to Washington.

The owners of the firm looked at each other with wide eyes. "Let's see how smoothly we can make this happen," one said to the other. "If we don't, we lose one hell of a customer. When does she need it, and what do we have in New Jersey?"

The first one checked his computer and looked up. "Well she's providing the muscle but not the driver, and she needs the box tomorrow. We're not supposed to know what's going in it, but apparently she's got some cargo that needs special handling. One day to load, one day to DC, and one day to unload. Did I mention that she's providing an armed guard who has his heavy rig license to ride shotgun? At some point he's going to take over and drive, so we won't be in at the end of the run. It's all being taken care of."

He checked some more. "Okay. We've got three empties in Newark but the only tractor is down for scheduled maintenance."

"Get it back up! This lady is important."

Another computer check.

"Ah, there's a tractor at the docks waiting for a late freighter. I can unhook it and use that one. Find a driver!"

Their phones were red hot for the next hour.

Melanie's trusted packers were actually security agents who worked for Protek. She needed them to pack the Cray and DJ's six other computers. They weren't happy about boxing and carrying DJ's items, but they did it for Melanie.

"Think of it as a different workout from your usual," she told them. "This cargo is very sensitive and I don't want anyone to know what it is or where it's going."

While she was dealing with the movers, contractors were already hard at work in a corner of the warehouse, hammering out a DC version of DJ's New Jersey apartment. Working from plans and photographs, they copied the layout—and even the paint colors—down to the last detail.

Holed up on the top floor of a nearby hotel, DJ suffered from a bad case of nerves, and that made him hungry. His only "fix"

was to place order after order of tacos and soda, which he wolfed down without tasting. He worried about his cats, so he kept calling Melanie for updates on Bam, Buzz, and Boo. He was told that his kitties were literally in the lap of luxury, being driven to DC in a limo by an expert driver whose wife sat in back petting them and feeding them treats.

Working with only one computer in his hotel, DJ became more agitated by the hour. The constant binging noise of emails from his irritated clients gave him a monster headache, reducing him to a state of almost complete paranoia. THEY knew where he was. THEY were coming to get him. NO ONE could help him now. He was DONE. His goose was COOKED.

He called room service and asked them to send up an order of French fries and a large Coke. After he ate, he calmed down for a little while and turned on the television to zone out.

"Damn," he said out loud to himself after a while. "Damn, damn, dammit to hell." He wasn't much of a thinker, but right now his brain was in overdrive. "This is what, Monday? When did I contact Ellen and Irving? Thursday night? So I met them on Friday. And here it is Monday and I'm in DC. Wow, these guys sure work fast! Wonder if they can fix this. Wonder if they can keep me alive...geez, I sure hope I did the right thing calling them."

He picked up the phone again and called Melanie to find out when he could move and when he could see Bam, Buzz, and Boo.

Melanie wrapped up the call with DJ and put the phone down. Add "kid sitter" to her ever-growing list of duties. To her, he was "the kid," but to some international-level hackers he was a man with a big target on his head and Melanie had two duties: protect his life and learn his secrets. When she did that, DJ's "clients" were going to have a very unpleasant time. She almost laughed. Five years ago she'd been unemployed and wondering what to do with her life. Now she was married, about to have a baby, and saving the world from international crime.

Then she really did laugh out loud.

The rig turned in to a truck stop just north of DC.

"This is good," said the driver. "I need to pee anyway."

When he got down, he was handed an envelope by his passenger.

He looked inside.

"Jesus!" he said, but the truck was already rolling.

He thought about calling the police, but then looked back into the envelope.

"I'll be damned," he said. He looked at the card inside with the cash. It said. "Remember the three monkeys— 'hear no evil, see no evil, and speak no evil'? Well, you will do the same thing. You didn't hear this rig, you didn't see this rig, and you damn well better not say anything about it."

He put the card back into the envelope, walked into the diner, and ordered coffee.

"Didn't you just get off that rig that drove away?" asked the waitress from behind the counter.

"No, that wasn't me. I never saw that rig before in my life."

Dom smiled as he pulled the big rig onto the highway. "Damn! I forgot how much fun these things are to drive."

Finally, the construction work was done and the next morning DJ was picked up at his hotel in a black sedan with tinted windows, which he pronounced "very cool." Mark drove the sedan around to the back of their office building, where the large garage door opened automatically and the car came to a stop in the middle of the indoor parking area. As the car door opened, DJ gasped at the sight of so many expensive, gleaming vehicles.

When Mark opened the door to DJ's newly built apartment, all DJ could do was whistle. Wow! There was his old place, right down to his favorite ratty chair, inside this super-cool garage. He didn't know where to look first—at the gleaming motorcycles parked right outside his door or inside, at his apartment.

Within seconds Melanie was at the door, greeting him. DJ, who had up until then spoken to her only by phone, was taken aback by the aura of power in this little lady who was obviously pregnant.

"Welcome, DJ," she said, extending her hand to him. "Your cats are waiting for you." She grinned. "And, lucky you, you won't have to change their kitty litter anymore. That will be taken care of for you as long as you keep working. Oh, and by the way, from now on you will take your orders from me."

DJ started to protest, "But they're *my* clients..."

"Yes, they are, DJ," interrupted Melanie, "but they are also master criminals, and moreover, they're after *you*. You may be a minor criminal in their arena, but you're a criminal, nevertheless. That's why you're here, remember? So we can protect you. Do you get it now, DJ? You will continue to make it *look* like you work for them, but from now on you will take your orders from me. I will tell you what you can and cannot do for them and even what to tell them—and *how* to tell them what is going on at your end."

He shuffled his feet and look at Melanie.

"In return," said Melanie firmly, "I will keep you *alive*, do you understand?"

He nodded and slyly eyed a powerful motorcycle out of the corner of his eye. He wondered if they would ever let him take it for a spin. Then, as if on cue, he walked into his apartment, found his cats sleeping on the sofa, and piled them all in his lap.

Melanie closed his front door and shook her head.

Chapter 13

Dee Gets to Work

SIMON WATSON STOOD ON THE cold sidewalk in front of Bart's law office and took another look at the check in his hands. He couldn't believe his good fortune. One day he was the owner of an art gallery he hated, and now, *now* he was *free*! Free to go anywhere and do anything he wanted. He'd come to hate this miserable gallery, especially the people who worked for him. Being the kind of person who had no self-awareness, Simon believed his employees had somehow turned on him. It never occurred to him that it was perhaps he himself who ruined their love of working at the gallery. Instead, he blamed the gallery's previous owner, thinking he'd been lied to about what a wonderful place it was.

***

High above the street, Dee, looking elegant in a black business suit, admired the view of the city from the conference room while having coffee with Bart.

"Bart, I can't thank you enough for all you've done for me."

"Always happy to help," replied Bart. "You know there's nothing I wouldn't do for the two of you."

There was a companionable silence for a few minutes while they sipped their coffee. One of Bart's assistants came in with more papers for Dee to sign. There was sales tax paperwork, a document to transfer the building's lease, vendor contracts, and more. Dee patiently signed them one by one, handing them back to Bart.

"Well, I guess my next stop is the gallery," she said, standing and shaking Bart's hand. "Won't everyone be surprised when they find out who the new owner is?"

Bart smiled and nodded. "Good luck, Dee. Call me if you need anything, okay?"

"I'll do that. Thanks again."

Across town at the gallery, there was a flurry of speculation. A few minutes ago a black sedan with tinted windows had pulled up in front of the building. The gentleman who came inside handed the manager a note requesting access to Simon's office to retrieve two boxes containing personal items. The request had been granted, and he was out of the gallery in two minutes. Now the only people who were there—the manager, the saleslady, and the stock boy—stood in the middle of the gallery wondering what had just happened. It didn't take long for them to find out.

Dee fairly jumped out of the cab. It was a moment she would never forget if she lived to be a hundred. Her dear friend Helen came running out of the gallery, her arms waving in the air, and flung herself at Dee.

"Oh my God, Dee, I can't believe you're here. I've missed you so much."

"I've missed you too, Helen. It's so good to see you. How are you?"

Helen grabbed her by the arm and pulled her into the gallery. "Look who's here! It's Dee. She used to be my manager. I *love* this lady!" She introduced Dee to the other two, who were too new at the gallery to know who she was.

Dee looked around, noticing the little things: windows that needed cleaning, dust in the corners, paintings with frames that didn't suit the style of the work. She was mentally cataloguing the work that needed to be done, while the three continued to chatter around her.

It was Helen who brought her back from her thoughts. "So, what brings you here today, Dee? It's a crazy day, anyway. Just now a stranger stopped by to pick up the owner's personal belongings, and now you show up. Crazy coincidence, right?"

"No coincidence," said Dee. "I'm the gallery's new owner."

Three chins dropped in unison, and the room grew as silent as a room can get when it fronts on New York City traffic.

Helen's grin lit up the room. "This calls for a *toast*," she all but shouted. "A toast to Dee!" And she ran to her office for the bottle she'd been saving for an occasion just like this.

The rest of the day flew by, as Dee worked with Helen to make the transition as smooth as possible. More than four years had passed since she'd left the gallery, and the trajectory had been downhill for most of that time. She had half a spiral notebook filled by the time she left there about four in the afternoon. Not only were revenues way down, the main issue was her customer base. Most of her beloved regulars had moved on to work with other galleries, and it wasn't going to be an easy task to win them back.

There was one stroke of luck. In a box in the storeroom she'd found some of her old records, thank goodness—forgotten, but not tossed out by the previous owner. Her "little black book" contained her customer records, and Dee was already formulating a plan to invite them to a cocktail party. But first she needed to take stock of what she had, clean the place up, and write a marketing plan. This was what she'd been waiting to do for so long; she couldn't wait to tell Jared about her day.

Half an hour and one cab ride later, she was climbing the stairs to their co-op on West Seventy-Sixth. She was so pleased to be able to do something as simple as take a cab ride home, which she hadn't been able to do for a while. Now, with Jonathan dead, and the threat to her life apparently over, Jared had eased up on his surveillance and protection of her. She knew he'd been with Bart in the afternoon and was on his way back to meet her. He kept in touch with her by cell phone throughout the day, always asking her to check in as she left one place or arrived at another. She decided it would be the perfect evening to have a cocktail and an early dinner at Tessa, which had become one of their favorite local restaurants.

It's just the right evening to be with someone you love, she thought, happily. Tonight Jared and I will celebrate, and tomorrow I'll get to work in earnest.

Helen welcomed her into her office the next day and they began to go over Dee's to-do list, item by item. As they delved into the details, Dee discovered that things were worse than she'd anticipated.

"First, clients," began Dee. Helen's body language told the whole story. They were basically down to the walk-ins and the tourists, all of their regular clientele having abandoned the gallery shortly after Dee left.

"I expected as much," she sighed. "Is there a chance of getting any of them back? I mean, they still live here, right? We could contact them? Have a cocktail party?"

"Not until we get some decent artists," came the quiet reply. "They have abandoned us too."

"No!"

"Yes, a long time ago."

The two old friends looked at each other for what seemed like forever, and then they broke into laughter—at the exact same time. They stood up and walked into the tiny kitchen in the back, and with two cups of dreadful coffee they proposed a toast: "To new beginnings," said Dee.

"To us, and to new beginnings," replied Helen.

And, in unison, "Now let's get to work."

Since Dee liked toys, on her first official lunch hour she found a computer store and bought herself a pink laptop. It would be hers and hers alone, not linked to any other computers in the gallery offices. To her that symbolized new beginnings, in her own way. She decided she would set up a new email address and a website of her own and would start to look for new artists. She would use the laptop for her ideas and her own special work.

The afternoon was devoted to going over the books, which was a depressing task. The only reason the gallery wasn't losing even more money was because they had cut expenses to the bone. That's why the gallery looked dirty—even the cleaning staff had been cut. She and Helen worked until six, when Jared stopped by to take both ladies to dinner.

In reality, Dee thought the best thing they could do for now was to close the gallery and open again once they were ready. She hated to do that at the holiday season, when they might actually make some sales. The three of them talked until late in the evening and parted as old friends, even though Jared had just met Helen.

"She's an older version of you, isn't she, Dee?" asked Jared, as they rode back to the Upper West Side in a cab.

"She is, and I guess that's what I've liked about her all along. You should hear the stories she tells about Simon. The man was truly diabolical. She was getting ready to abandon ship. Another week or two and I wouldn't even have found her at the gallery. She tells me all she wanted was to go back to Dayton, job or no job. Sad. I'm so happy I did this, Jared. No, let me correct that: so happy *we* did this!"

He hugged her a little closer.

By the end of the first week, Dee was back in gear. The windows and the floors had been cleaned, and the few paintings that were still in stock had been rehung to better advantage. They were getting a handle on planning and budgeting.

On Friday afternoon, a lone woman wandered in.

"May I help you?"

"Just looking, thanks," came the reply, but the woman was glancing around as though she had something specific in mind.

"Did I hear you're under new management?"

Helen responded, "We are, actually, but I don't think there's any way you would have heard about it. No announcement's been made."

"Well, I'm a bit of a collector myself. I'm always looking for good paintings, especially by European artists. Since I travel on business, when I fly in from Boston, I'll make sure to stop by to see how things are going."

Hairs stood up on the back of Helen's neck at the way the woman said that, and she made a mental note to mention it to Dee.

But then she got busy again and it slipped her mind.

Two blocks away in a luncheonette, Mary Rose ordered black coffee and snapped open her phone. "Talk," came the terse reply.

"I've found her, Papa. I know where she is."

"Good, Maria. That was good work, finding her. But do not touch her, okay? It's enough that we know where she is."

"I know, Papa. Do not pet the cobra, am I right?"

Joseph sighed and signed off in Italian, "Arrevaderchi."

Meanwhile, back in her office, Dee typed away on her laptop. She'd already entered all of her old clients into a spreadsheet she could sort several different ways. She'd ask Helen's sales assistant to look it over to see if the phone numbers and addresses were current. Dee knew how rapidly the art scene changed in New York, so she decided her market plan would focus on finding new artists. She even thought about "going undercover," a la Las Vegas, and paying visits to her old competitors. She made a mental note to ask Jared if he liked the idea. While she was at it, she made competitor lists as well and asked Helen if her assistant could also print up their latest websites and put them in a notebook with tabs.

She wanted to hold her first show in a month, and she knew it was almost an impossibility—unless, she thought, she could get the artists to send her samples of their work to display at the opening; going any other route could take months. So she began with the websites she knew, like Novica and Etsy, and contacted artist after artist. By the end of the day she was already receiving answers. That was the most exciting thing that had happened to her all week. It was a longshot, but it could work. She promised to pay the artists for packing and shipping, and their responses were overwhelmingly positive.

One more idea came to mind; the gallery needed a new name: something short, sophisticated, and easy to remember. Once she had the name, a graphic artist she knew could design the logo, the signage, business cards, pens, and notepads. Her mind raced with ideas. This is what she had been missing, and now she had it back!

It was Friday night of her first week, and Dee was elated. Jared was on his way to pick her up, and they were going up to the country for a long weekend.

Chapter 14

DJ's Crash Course

D J's DAYS OF TAKING THINGS at his own pace were over.
All his time was scheduled with meetings, debriefings,
and training. Melanie was definitely in charge now.

At 8 a.m. the next morning, Melanie had one of her staff
knock at DJ's door and escort him to his first meeting. This was
not what DJ had expected when he asked Ellen and Irving for
protection. The questioning began. Melanie wanted the names,
email addresses, and history of each one of his clients, along
with a complete description of what DJ did for each of them,
where they were in the process, and, most important, what he
knew of their plans. Melanie wanted her takeover to be seamless.
For that, she had to know everything there was to know. She had
to get inside DJ's mind.

It took her all day to sort through the mess.

DJ might be a 'crack hacker,' thought Melanie, but his mind
wandered something awful, and she had a tough time keeping
him on course. He constantly strayed off the track, talking about
video games, his mother, his cats…God, talk about ADHD, the
list was endless. Melanie recorded it all and then pulled in an
assistant to capture all the details in a spreadsheet to make sure
they weren't missing anything.

Meanwhile, she had to give DJ a break every hour or so, so
he could go back to his new apartment and monitor the emails
that came in at breakneck speed all day—*and all night*—long.
No wonder DJ was frazzled. Melanie was by now pretty sure

his contacts were worldwide. It was easy to see that he could have contacts in Russia, given the middle-of-the-night timing of many of the emails.

For the present, Melanie had told DJ to placate his clients until she could determine the best way to turn them around. And, to be able to do that, she would have to have a firm grasp on all of his "projects"—as she had taken to calling them. It was not fun, and Baby Boy was kicking her for most of the day, leaving her tired and irritable. She was happy Mitch would be home tonight. She was going to need some babying herself, she thought.

At home that evening, Melanie took it easy for the first time all day. That is if you could call it relaxing with Baby Boy doing summersaults in her midsection. Her feet were up, they'd eaten a takeout dinner, and she had extra pillows stuffed behind her back.

"As near as I can tell," Melanie told Mitch as he massaged her feet, "there are five—let's call them—subjects. DJ digresses more than he talks, which drives me crazy, but eventually I can start to put it together."

"These subjects," Mitch countered, "can you get a handle on them yet? I mean, enough information to identify them and determine where they are?"

"Well," Melanie continued, "there's Pretty Boy. DJ talks about him a lot. He emails all day long, which, to my mind, puts him in the same time zone. Then there's Evil Eye, who I think lives on the west coast. He works with someone else, so I'm putting these two together. I think they are techies from Silicon Valley; maybe they were fired by the company they worked for, so they turned against the establishment. I've taken to calling them the Surfer Dudes."

"Great start," said Mitch, "but I thought there was an overseas connection too."

"There is," she continued, "they are the ones who email DJ all night long. He calls them 'Boris and Natasha,' but I doubt they are man and woman—more likely, they are Boris and Ivan." From the way DJ reacts to their emails, I think they're the ringleaders. For sure they are the ones he's most afraid of—and they send him loads of threatening emails."

Melanie continued, "These five are the key players in the credit card scams. And from the way DJ has been sweating, I know things have escalated in the past day or two. If they are all working together, they could pull off a scam large enough to threaten the world's major retailers and banks right in time for Christmas." She exhaled slowly; Mitch was silent for a while. Melanie knew when he was thinking, so she let her body relax and waited for him to say something.

"Okay, so even if we can get the ones who live in the US—we will need to find and 'deactivate' the other two. If they are outside the country, it's not going to be easy—unless we hatch a plot to get them to come to us." Melanie's eyes opened wide, and then she laughed.

"I see where you're going with this. Interesting…Do you think Jared's up for an evening conference call? I think it's time we filled him in on what's happening."

Later, after they'd talked to Jared, Melanie had to admit she agreed with him: it was time for DJ to get his proverbial head out of his proverbial ass.

"Jared doesn't usually swear," said Melanie, "but this time he's right on target. I'm calling DJ right now to tell him to have his butt back in my office at 8 a.m. tomorrow for a full staff meeting. We are going to get to the bottom of this—and quickly.

I am getting some bad vibes. There's no time to spare and we have a lot of work to do."

———————

It was late at night, but Jared still had two more calls to make. First he dialed Joseph's number; he knew that he would answer.

"Joseph, I need to ask you something."

"Talk, Jared," came the reply, but it was softer and lacking in authority.

"There's a flurry of Internet activity, indicating that something big—something very big—is going to come down in the next few days. If you hear anything, could you let me know?"

"I'll get back to you, Jared. Tomorrow?"

"That will be fine. Are you doing okay, Joseph?"

"It's not easy. It's not easy at all. I'm an old man."

"You take care. Goodnight, Joseph. And thank you."

His second call went to an after-hours number where he knew a federal agent would be monitoring the phone. Jared quickly told him that he was harboring a known criminal, a hacker, who was wanted by the feds on several charges.

"Tell your boss I'll call him tomorrow and explain what's going on."

"Thanks," came the reply. "Will do, and good night, Jared."

Chapter 15

The Planning Meeting

As requested, DJ was in Melanie's conference room by eight the next morning. Although he looked scruffy and kept running his hands through his untrimmed hair, he was there and ready to work. Melanie had cleared the decks and called an all-hands meeting. She watched as Ellen and Irving arrived looking almost as unscrubbed as DJ, but they seemed alert and ready to work. Melanie, fit as ever, had dressed in yoga pants and a tight purple tee that made her watermelon-sized belly look even larger than usual. And there was one newcomer in the mix—hastily invited the night before—Jared's baby-faced financial hero from Bart's law firm, James Blake III. Melanie called him Mr. Preppy, but not to his face. The date, she noted, for her agenda, was November 12, 2008.

"Team," she began, "we are here to plan and carry out the largest and most complicated security mission our company has ever been faced with. Until we solve this case, there will be no other priorities but this one. Is that clear?" Heads nodded all around the table; laptops snapped open, almost in unison.

Melanie continued, "This is what we have so far. We have reason to believe DJ's 'clients' are planning a huge operation that will target the major US credit card companies and shopping malls in time for Christmas shopping. While DJ is their main operative, they have not shared everything with him yet. It's obvious they need him, since he's one of the best hacker-programmers in the business—but it's my opinion that

93

they don't trust him completely. They appear to be feeding him information on a need-to-know basis."

Melanie looked around the table. DJ was toying with his laptop, but his eyes were fixed on Ellen's chest. Melanie, noting his distraction, snapped her fingers in his direction, and he looked up, a guilty expression plastered on his face.

James spoke up. "If they are going to skim credit cards, as I presume they are, then they are most likely targeting Black Friday. It's the biggest shopping day of the year."

"My thoughts exactly," replied Melanie. "That gives us two weeks to put a counterattack initiative into place. If anyone has made plans to go home for Thanksgiving, please cancel them now. Once we solve this case, I'll make sure you all get a belated holiday—at company expense. Meanwhile, good thinking, James. Thank you."

In his earlier debriefing with Melanie, DJ indicated he usually had almost no warning when something big was coming down. Sometimes the orders were confusing, and even, at times, contradictory. The emails would come after a period of relative quiet and would start with requests for programming changes, usually to an old project. Sometimes it would be Boris: "Hey little boy-o. Run us 100K of clean names. Update old list, then sit tight, okay?" That was DJ's signal to ramp up the Cray and update his database of stolen credit cards that he could activate if need be. At other times it could be Pretty Boy, emailing DJ with information on what was going on at various retail outlets, with warnings to be prepared. Sometimes the California boys were merely copied on these messages, and no one knew if they worked or if they surfed all day long.

Melanie gave everyone a break so they could get coffee and power bars from the side table and then continued. "Here's how I see the roles playing out. DJ, since you are the criminals' main contact, you will continue to work with them as if nothing has changed. The only difference is that now I will be running *you*. Ellen and Irving, you will hack into the criminals' systems and keep me informed about what they are up to. Can you do that without their knowing you are onto them?" Both of them nodded.

Ellen looked at Irving, raising an eyebrow. "We might need some help, Melanie," she offered. "It'll be three of them to two of us, even if you count their two's as one's. Can we have Karen? I'll hack into Pretty Boy, Irving can have the foreigners, and Karen can watch over the Surfer Dudes. We can show her what she needs to do, and then supervise her. Will that be okay?" Melanie immediately agreed and asked to have Karen join the meeting.

That left James. "James, I am putting you in charge of the entire banking operation. Can you handle it?" He nodded, sitting a little straighter. "Excellent, I thought so," continued Melanie. "Give me your requirements, preferably in database format, of what you will need in the way of banking information, and the rest of the team will start feeding it to you as they get it, okay?"

At this point James spoke up again. "May I offer a little explanation? I learned something about this in business school." Melanie smiled, encouraging him to go on.

"Here is what DJ is going to have to do," James began. "This is not intended to ruin the American economy. It is a textbook scam to make a few people very rich in a very short time. The basic premise is to skim pennies from billions of credit and debit card transactions and divert them to their own accounts." James paused. "That is what 'The Penny Scam' is."

He had their rapt attention and continued to outline how the scam worked. "Normally, when a customer makes a purchase using a credit or debit card, the amount is instantly transmitted to the bank of reference, which immediately credits the store's account."

Gesturing in DJ's direction, he said, "DJ has learned how to program in filters that add pennies to the purchase and sales tax amounts, so that when the stores are credited, the store gets the actual purchase amount, and the pennies show up on the customer's bill. The customer pays the bill to the bank at the end of the month and pays the pennies. So, the customer is the one who actually pays for the scam. Good, so far?"

There were nods from various people around the conference table.

"So, in order to counter the scam, DJ has rewritten the software so the pennies can be diverted on the way up. We are the diversion. We make sure they never get to the card companies or the banks. The customers never see them on their bills. They have become *imaginary pennies*. They seem to show up on accounts that DJ and I have set up for Boris and Natasha, but they don't exist, and those accounts, although they seem to be growing pennies, are actually zero. Our real task is keeping up with the flow so they can't get around us, because there are thousands of stores and hundreds of millions of transactions.

"The good news is that they funnel through relatively few channels to the financial hubs. It's going to be a busy day, and if they get a hint that we're in the mix, it's going to hit the fan. Any questions?" James asked.

"Why are we doing this—sending the fake pennies out to Boris and Natasha's accounts?" asked one of the meeting participants.

"Because we want to nail their hides to the barn door so this kind of scam can never happen again," said Melanie.

There were a few more technical questions, but they were quickly answered. At this point, they were less than one hour into the meeting, and there were nods all around. Melanie, as usual, had chopped a huge task into bite-sized pieces, making it manageable for the team. In fact, she was already closing the meeting.

"Good work, everyone. Please have the operating plan for your role on my desk by close of business today. I need to review them side by side to see what we're missing. It's not like we're going to have time for a do-over. This is going down in two weeks, and we'd better get it right."

By the next morning Melanie thought she had a handle on things. She was tired, having been awake most of the night, first reviewing the team's plans and then suffering through foot and leg cramps that required her to jump out of bed every twenty minutes and hop from one foot to another until they went away. She joined the group via her laptop and let Ellen run the office end of the meeting. Jared joined them by video. He indicated he'd also been up half the night, and reported to the team the results of his phone and video meetings with executives of the credit card companies, banks, and department store chains he'd been able to reach. They were, he reported, on board, and eager to receive assistance from his elite team. They were also worried, given that they stood to lose millions—maybe hundreds of millions—in legal fees trying to reimburse their customers if the operation failed. Jared had assured them this wouldn't happen.

Now it was up to his team to guarantee it.

Chapter 16

The Takedown

F OR THE REST OF THE country it was Thanksgiving. But for Melanie's team, it was an exhausting workday. Sure, containers of turkey and mashed potatoes had been brought in, but the Styrofoam containers and their goodies took second place to a slew of ongoing activities. Technicians were networking DJ's computers to the ones in the communications center, and all the equipment was being tested, first by the techs and then by the users themselves. Everyone was being fitted with headsets and microphones so they could stay in verbal contact as well. Even a low-tech whiteboard was being installed on the wall of the communications center, and one of Melanie's assistants was gathering and distributing supplies.

Melanie had to have one last talk with DJ. First and foremost, she needed to grab his attention and try to focus it on the task at hand. "DJ, I want you to know you're safe with us. You will work better if your mind is clear, and you can stop thinking that 'they' are coming to get you. Are you with me on this?"

He was silent for a moment and then looked at Melanie and nodded. "I've been afraid for so long—especially of Boris and Natasha—that it will be hard to do. But I'll try."

Melanie continued, "No one knows you're here. If anyone thinks they know where you are, they would look for you in New Jersey, right?"

A little smile came over his face. "Yeah, right. And I'm not in New Jersey anymore, am I? Where am I again, Melanie?"

"You're at Protek headquarters in Washington, DC, DJ, and you're safe with us. This building is the best-kept secret in town—probably safer even than the Pentagon." That got his attention.

"Wow, neat. Thanks for telling me."

"Plus, this building has twenty-four-hour security, so even if anyone did know what was going on, they would never be able to penetrate our installations."

He looked worried. "Will I still get my takeout deliveries?"

"Of course. All of our fast food vendors have been vetted—and cleared."

"Good." That seemed to satisfy him.

She shifted gears and began to walk him through the actual plan, working from her notes, which had, in turn, come from each team member's operational plans. There was a lot to think about, and she didn't want to miss anything, because when it started, everything was going to happen quickly—and there couldn't be any mistakes.

Thanksgiving afternoon turned into early evening in Washington, DC, and even though the rest of the country was watching football and falling asleep on couches, Melanie's team was going full-tilt. In fact, at about 7 p.m., Melanie called a collective break, telling everyone to find a comfy couch or chair and to "sack out" for a little while. The entire setup was now in place.

She had her own laptop mapped to monitor DJ's incoming mail, so no one was more surprised than she when the emails started pouring in at about 8:30 p.m. She was on her headset to DJ in a flash.

"DJ, are you awake? It's starting."

"Yes, ma'am, I'm awake."

"I'll be right over, DJ."

All over the building, people and computers were springing into action.

Melanie watched over DJ's shoulder.

"Hey, pip-squeak, we got a little job for you to do…you there?"

"Affirmative," replied DJ.

This was followed by a string of instructions from overseas, which were showing up simultaneously on Ellen and Irving's screens in the command center, so they could follow the proceedings.

Melanie, who had never seen DJ in action before, stood mesmerized behind his chair as he went into overdrive. His fingers flew, and more than one of his laptops was churning out work already. She ran out of his apartment and into the command center and saw the exact same level of intensity from Ellen and Irving. James, she noted, was watching and accompanying the start-up proceedings. She recognized that the bulk of his work would come later.

Everyone was momentarily too busy to tell her what was going on. She tried to follow the action, but for the next hour or so, she moved rapidly—well, as rapidly as she could—from one operation to the other, making sure no one needed anything. She brought coffee for Ellen and Irving and called in an order of tacos for DJ.

She was amazed at DJ's speed and intensity. Was it the talk she'd had with him, or was this the "real DJ" in action? Before she knew it, it was 10 p.m., and she knew no one would get much sleep. She called Mitch and asked him to come to the office to keep her company. He was there in ten minutes. The love of my life, thought Melanie, and she felt so much better knowing he was there.

It soon became obvious that Boris and Natasha were the main operators, and the target was as expected: the hordes of Black

Friday shoppers and their gold, platinum, and titanium credit cards—AMEX, MasterCard, VISA—all of which were going through a "bypass filter" ordered by Boris and implemented by DJ. Every credit card purchase made in the US, beginning at 10 p.m. and continuing throughout the next shopping day, would have a small fee added to it, in the form of a tiny sales tax increment, a minimally inflated price, or any other number of tricks DJ had programmed in. With this many plays up his sleeve, it would be hard, under normal circumstances, to catch such a thief. And, worse yet, the individual amounts were so tiny that customers most likely would never notice the variation—unless they were looking for it—and of course, they weren't. It was the "perfect storm" of credit card scams. Pick the biggest shopping day of the year and skim pennies off millions and millions of individual card transactions.

Melanie thought Boris and Natasha must be sitting back and thinking they had the whole damn world by the tail right about now.

Melanie watched spellbound as DJ settled in to a pattern that seemed totally familiar to him. He answered Boris and Natasha, giving as good as he got.

"Okay, you weasels," wrote DJ, "the AMEX transactions are coming in at the rate of ninety thousand customers an hour, you greedy bastards."

Boris fired back, "Fack you, pip-squeak. Keep working, or we kill you!"

DJ, apparently feeling safe under Melanie's protection, hooted with laughter and fired another equally noxious email back at Boris.

Shaking her head, Melanie tore herself away from DJ's apartment and ran back to the command center. Ellen and Irving were working at the same pace as DJ, trying to keep up with what Boris and Natasha were doing behind the scenes. Then

Irving walked over to James for a quick chat, while Ellen sent him a stream of numbers.

Melanie could see that James had started to dummy up the fake bank balances to feed to Boris and Natasha. The numbers he received from Ellen allowed him to make some educated guesses as to the amounts to input into the fake online bank accounts that the two would access.

Melanie watched, on and off, all night, while her team performed the most amazingly difficult tasks at breakneck speed. She'd never been prouder of them. Once in a while Mitch made her get off her feet, and he massaged them. He fed her healthy snacks and made sure she stayed hydrated, while he kept her up to date.

The work continued all through Friday. Everyone took short rests and covered for each other. Melanie took over DJ's role every few hours so he could take a break. She was getting pretty good at emulating his nasty emails to Boris and Natasha. If it weren't so serious, it might even be fun, she thought to herself.

By about 11 p.m. on Friday, most of the stores on the east coast of the US were closing their doors and tallying their sales, which had been good, by all accounts. Customers eager to get great deals on clothing, computers, and jewelry, had used their credit cards like true red-blooded American consumers. Credit card companies were doing the same thing. The volume of business had been huge, perhaps even record breaking.

And only a few executives in the business knew what had been happening for the past twenty-four hours.

Melanie's shop was in disarray. Food and drink containers and wrappers covered almost every surface. Her peeps were running totals and comparing notes. Some merely sat back and closed their eyes for a few minutes.

Sometime during the late afternoon Mitch had alerted the FBI that it was time to pick up Pretty Boy and the Surfer

Dudes. Ellen and Irving had been able to physically locate them during the night, so they were now out of commission and being questioned by the feds.

All the money was safely back in the banks' accounts, with their teams of accountants, both internal and external, poring over the transactions, and, among other things, calculating Protek's fee.

The numbers were staggering. It turned out to be the largest scam-busting operation of its kind—ever. And no one but a handful of people even knew about it. The press never got even a sniff of scandal. If they had, of course, they would have had a field day. But, no, that didn't happen.

Far away on another continent, Boris and Natasha were unaware that they had been busted and they didn't even notice that their colleagues were offline. They were too busy watching what they thought were their bank accounts being filled to overflowing with American dollars scammed from the credit card accounts of the American capitalists. It wasn't until much later that they found out one man in Melanie's shop was responsible for that particular sleight of hand.

Gleefully they went to bed thinking they were rich. It wasn't until Monday morning that they learned the truth—and their fate.

They were in deep trouble and about to take a hastily arranged trip.

Chapter 17

Happy Belated Thanksgiving

I**T WASN'T YOUR TYPICAL** "**MORNING** after." For the rest of the country it was a day to drag yourself back to work after a four-day Thanksgiving weekend. It was also Cyber Monday, a day when turkey-fueled office workers would rather shop online than attend meetings. But, for Melanie's team, it was mop-up day after a busy and successful operation. Melanie let everyone sleep in and called her meeting for 9 a.m. instead of eight. There was grumbling, because most of them had not slept more than four hours a night for the past week. Some, still too tired to come in, called in on the conference line.

"Team," Melanie began at 9:05, "a huge 'well done' to all of you. You performed your tasks admirably, and the operation has been a complete success. Well, almost," she trailed off, "but we will get back to that later."

"Here are the main points," she continued. "Our five bad guys were going for a billion-dollar takedown. They would have come close if we hadn't intervened. Their actual 'take'—which they didn't actually *take*, of course—was 948 million dollars. That included one extremely lucky east coast shopping mall chain and three major banks, with all of their credit card products."

A collective "aahhhhh" escaped the lips of those in the room, plus the ones on speaker phone.

"All of that money has been returned to its rightful owners, minus our fee," stated Jared. "And we do have some grateful and relieved executives who now believe in the power of Protek's financial security team. Word is quickly and quietly spreading around the industry as we speak."

"Melanie," asked Ellen, "what has happened with our perps? Were Mark and Mitch in on that end?"

Mark came on the line himself. "Surfer Dudes and Pretty Boy are eating breakfast provided by the feds this morning. They still don't know how they got nabbed. We have one more issue to resolve. Can anyone guess what it is?"

Karen volunteered, "Boris and Natasha?"

"Right," came Mark's reply, "and we have a plan—providing everyone is willing to hold off on Thanksgiving for a few more days. And, DJ, we are going to need your help—and your mother's—to finish this. Is everyone in?"

Next, Melanie held a closed-door meeting with only Mitch and Mark.

"Because of his so-called lifestyle, DJ and his mom are usually at odds," Melanie explained, "except once a month, when Mom calls a truce. You may have heard she threw him out when he was eighteen and got him his own apartment because she couldn't deal with him. She's a high-powered attorney who lives in an elegant, turn-of-the-century house on a hill in Westbush, New Jersey. On the first Sunday of the month, she opens her door to him and lovingly serves him dinner, just like she did when he was a little boy. And DJ has bought into it—he's never missed a Sunday since she threw him out."

The two guys shook their heads and chuckled.

"It's not funny," said Melanie, "but it does afford us the perfect opportunity to catch Boris and his sidekick. Guess what this coming Sunday is?"

Two pairs of eyes widened and looked at Melanie, who nodded and smirked. "Yup, first Sunday of the month and DJ's belated Thanksgiving dinner. And, there's one more thing to take into account..."

Later that same day Melanie called Jared and he agreed with her idea. "Let me know if you need any additional resources," he told her. She began to put her latest plan in motion. By the time she'd put this one to bed, she decided, she would put her feet up—and they would stay up—until after Christmas.

Gladys Owen, Attorney at Law, DJ's mother, graciously welcomed her new clients into her office. They were a pleasant looking couple and apparently important, since she'd received a call from a colleague named Bart who told her to 'fit them in today' no matter who she had to bump.

"How may I help you?" she asked with a solicitous air.

"It's about your son DJ," said Jared, coming right to the point.

"Not again!" she blurted. "That boy will be the death of me! Sometimes I wish I'd kept my legs crossed. What's he done now?" Then she realized how unprofessional that sounded and immediately apologized.

"Actually," said Dee, "this time he's gotten himself into something beneficial to our economy."

"What?" Gladys gulped and then silenced herself while Jared spent the next half hour explaining what had happened over the past weekend. At the end, she stood up and started to pace back and forth while she digested all she'd heard.

"Is DJ going to jail? I will obviously have to recuse myself from defending him for personal reasons, but I have friends who would do it…"

Jared held up his hand. "He's not going to jail. It will never come to that. Yes, he did skim pennies off credit card sales, but this time he was working for us, and not the bad guys. He even donated his—shall we call them 'commissions'—to charity, hoping this would help find a cure for the disease that killed his little sister. Then he hacked back in and put the money in a tax write-off fund for the credit card companies. They're making tiny adjustments to all the customer accounts and calling it a bonus. It cost millions of pennies, but nobody missed it and so far everyone is cool with it. Now, we did have to put pressure on the FBI to keep them from coming down here first to muscle you into helping us before we could find out if you were willing to do it, but they went along with us."

Gladys glared at Jared. "Who exactly *are* you?" she asked, pointedly.

"We are a privately owned security company, and we have been involved with this case from the beginning. In fact, we were the ones who informed and brought in the FBI and the other agencies when it all went down. They weren't happy, but they realized Protek has the talent and the inside information. Now it's mop-up time—and you can help us."

"Is my son safe?" she asked.

"Yes, but he doesn't live in New Jersey anymore. Let's say he's in a place that looks remarkably like his old home with his computers and his cats."

She looked at Dee and Jared. They could see her mind working. Finally, she came to a decision. "What do I have to do?"

Em and Henry began packing their bags for the weekend.

"This is going to be fun," said Em. "Time for a little playacting."

"Playacting, my eye," said Henry. "Time for some action! Been sitting on the sidelines for too long. I want to whack some people over their heads and tie them up!"

Boris, whose real first name was Ivan, was a fine figure of a man at 190 cm and 100 kilos. In his youth he had placed first wrestling in the 100-kilo class in the Kiev games. He was still at that weight at twenty-nine years of age. He was big but not handsome, and with his flat face and sloped forehead he looked rather stupid. But behind the face was a brain that considered hacking into highly secure computer networks the same as playing video games.

Boris's father had been an operative in the Cold War, stationed in Annapolis, Maryland, where he was supposed to study and report on the training methods the US Navy used for their cadets at the academy. As it turned out, the first thing he learned was that Americans were friendly and liked to drink, as did he, so camaraderie flowed along with the beer. The other thing he learned was that the training was much more rigorous and disciplined than what he'd seen in the Ukraine. As an example, along with marching and classes, as part of the hazing, the new cadets had to memorize and learn a folksong called "Abdul, the Bulbul Amir" (all eighteen verses) and be prepared to sing it whenever an upper classman bid them do it. Boris's father loved it because the song was about a duel between Abdul and a Russian named 'Ivan Skavinsky Skivar.' Since Boris's father's name was Skivar, he learned the song and sang it with the cadets in a Russian accent. It earned him many free shots of vodka. And his patronymic was also Ivanovich, which added to the lore.

When he was recalled home to his beloved Lyudmila, in a vodka moment he decided what to name his firstborn son.

His son never forgave him.

—————————⟡—————————

Natasha, born Natalia Petrovskyia, had always wanted to be a ballerina. But when she grew past 170 cm and 39 kilos, she knew it wasn't going to work. The boys couldn't pick her up over their heads anymore. Then they started to tease her, cruelly. They called her 'the dumb bell'—there for them to work out with and gain upper body strength. Not to dance with. The more they laughed at her, the more her hatred of men coalesced. Finally, one of the boys took his insults too far—and she broke his leg.

He would never dance again.

Of course, she was brought to a disciplinary tribunal—all old men. Hope disintegrated in her heart. The first judge recommended that she be shipped off to a commune to drive a tractor and grow wheat for the rest of her life. She was, after all, a strong, healthy, and growing young Ukrainian woman. "What better use for her?"

The second judge disagreed. "Have you looked at her scholastic records, Tovatishchi? She is a genius with computers. She writes video games for fun. She should go into our cyber war group."

The third judge agreed, but for a different reason: she was not only intelligent, she was beautiful and a talented gymnast. With a little redirection, she could excel in martial arts. She was also vicious. All of which made her a rare commodity.

So Natasha was given a new name and went to a new academy where she learned new dance steps. She was partnered with Boris, whom she could almost stand, both for his physique and his computer skills. She did put him in his place at the onset of their relationship when he tried to grope her left breast. He wound up with his face plastered against the wall and his arm held painfully behind his back.

"Don't ever try that again!" she whispered, pushing it a little farther to emphasize her point.

Natasha knew how to hurt men so they would tell her anything she wanted to know.

Yes, indeed, that was her strong suit.

Now, Boris was angry. He couldn't figure out what had gone

wrong with their operation the weekend before. The key had to be this little asshole, DJ. The man Boris worked for, the Iceman, had told Boris and his partner, Natasha, to get their asses on an Aeroflot flight to Heathrow and then on to JFK to grab the little geek.

So off they went.

Mitch's radio crackled into action. "Suspects' plane has landed. We will get our first look at our two subjects as soon as they get in line at US Customs. It will probably take them an hour to get through the line and then another half hour to get clear, so ETA today is 4 p.m."

Everyone agreed, and Mitch continued.

Tomorrow is turkey day—ETA for that is 3:30 p.m. Will everything be ready for that too?"

"Affirmative for the turkey," came Melanie's voice over the radio. "Too bad it isn't a goose. I would love to be able to say 'their goose is cooked.' Keep me posted when they clear customs, okay?"

As it turned out, they were a day late and a dollar short.

Mark slipped his earphones off and returned to his surveillance. He was located in an observation room high above the US Customs arrival zone. With him were two FBI agents, one airport official, the airport's highest-ranking customs officer, and his own communications assistant. All eyes were peeled on the latest arrivals on the last flight from Heathrow on Saturday.

Mark had almost nothing to go on. He had no idea what the perpetrators looked like. He wasn't even sure whether he was looking for two men or a man and a woman. The FBI agents weren't much help—all they had were a few grainy photos and generic descriptions of some known cyber criminals.

For once Melanie had screwed up badly. She didn't think they would show up before Saturday; instead, they had flown in on Friday and checked into a local hotel. She had her team looking for two males, and the male/female team slipped under her radar. Besides, these two were scheduled on a flight to Philadelphia to attend a Special Olympics conference. How bad could they be? As it turned out—it was very bad.

Boris and his partner couldn't believe what they were seeing. The US was very different from what they had been told. There were nice cars everywhere; the people were friendly; there was joy and happiness at this holiday season! It was overwhelming. So they settled in at the Westbush Inn and got their emails telling them what to do and where to collect the tools they would need to snatch DJ. Like Hans and Georg, they thought this would be easy. They made the same mistaken assumption.

DJ's mother's home was an elegant residence by anyone's standards, and it sat way back on a large corner lot, surrounded by trees. Of course at this time of year, those trees were bare, and passersby who looked in the windows would think something festive was in progress. It should have been a scene from a holiday movie or a magazine: a perfectly designed kitchen with apple and pumpkin pies decorating the counter, happy people chatting while the turkey cooked, and lovely smells filling the entire house. Gladys was entertaining Em and Henry, who were role playing as her own mother and father. Irving, made up as DJ, had just been driven in from Newark Airport.

Irving was amused that Gladys did a perfect double take when she realized he wasn't DJ.

"It's wonderful what they can do with makeup," remarked Em.

"Who are you?" Gladys asked, looking directly at Irving.

"My name is Irving," he replied, "aka DJ. We are keeping the real DJ safe and sound. I happen to look enough like him that I was 'volunteered' for the job. I'm his stand-in stunt man."

Henry almost choked.

Irving had been prepped by Melanie, with a simple reminder: "Irving, whatever happens, go along with it. You are simply acting as DJ going home for a belated Thanksgiving dinner. Don't try to be a hero, and, if necessary, keep your head down! We all love you and want you to come back to us safe and sound."

Irving thought maybe Melanie was getting overly maudlin because of her pregnancy, so he let it slide. "Nice to hear it," he said, and then thought about Ellen and realized the team was truly concerned about him. He squared his shoulders, which wouldn't have passed a Marine muster, but it made him feel better anyway.

The real problem with this wonderful scene was that Gladys couldn't successfully boil water, much less cook an entire Thanksgiving dinner. When DJ showed up for their monthly Sunday dinner they often called out for pizza or tacos, the two major food groups necessary for sustenance, as far as DJ was concerned. Oh, and soda, in various brands. So Gladys had called the best local catering service and ordered an entire Thanksgiving dinner, specialty colas, and a good German wine to go with the turkey. They were due to arrive in an hour.

Gladys was amazed to find out that Auntie Em and Henry weren't quite the country bumpkins she'd expected. Em had a master's degree in English and Henry had a bachelor's in mechanical engineering with a minor in philosophy. They were also deputy sheriffs with a good deal of experience in justice, which impressed Gladys. Apparently, jail time was not the primary punishment in upstate New York, except when a major crime had been committed. Otherwise, you spent a couple of days in Sandra's single jail cell eating the worst food the cooks across the street could make—and Sandra told them when to make it *bad*. After you were charged and convicted, everyone in the county knew about it—that was the worst punishment of all.

They watched you.

Peer pressure.

"Don't do it again!"

And it worked—until Jonathan moved in—but now that he was gone things were back to normal.

Gladys thought, if only she could make that work in Newark. But then she got realistic and shook her head.

The cocktail hour sped by with these stories until Gladys began to wonder what was taking the caterers such a long time.

Fred and his partner loaded up the van with Gladys's turkey dinner, which he estimated would be on her table in thirty minutes, and he would take home a generous tip.

As they drove out of the lot, however, there was a pickup truck blocking the road. Fred hit the horn and rolled down his window. As he was about to shout, a large man wearing a white jacket materialized from behind him and put a gun to his head. He was dragged out of the truck and bound with plastic wire ties. The passenger-side door was similarly pulled open and an armed woman dragged the other man out of the van, pistol-whipping him across the face. Blood spurted and he collapsed on the ground. She rolled him over and bound him too.

Boris looked at Natasha with disgust.

"Сукой!" he said, "Why did you pistol-whip him? Do you think you are going to serve dinner in a bloody jacket?"

"Пошел на хуй!" she retorted.

Boris threw her Fred's coat and told her to put it on and shut up. "No guns," he reminded her. "We have to take the little nerd alive. Now, move the damn pickup."

She gave him an unladylike gesture and did as she was told.

Boris thought that as soon as he got to DJ's Cray the rest would be easy. Then he could dump the bitch.

Now, on a quiet Sunday afternoon in Westbush, a team of more than two dozen people was in place, not to mention all the high-tech equipment Melanie had loaded into a semi and sent up from Washington, DC. She'd included communications equipment as well as several vehicles she thought would work to their advantage—even a motorcycle and an ambulance! The rig was parked downtown in Trader Joe's parking lot, and the driver was hanging out next door in Panera's waiting for instructions.

Melanie was too far along in her pregnancy to travel, but Mitch was there at the command center—a heating and air conditioning repair truck parked half a block down the street with a good view and field of fire to Gladys's house. Dom had come along with them. Melanie was always looking for special talent that some had and most didn't—physical toughness and heads-up intelligence to make instant decisions. It was, in her opinion, a rare combination, and Dom had it.

Dom sat in the truck alongside Mitch and Mark. Although it wasn't much of a job, he'd managed the move of DJ's apartment from New Jersey to DC, even driving the semi the last twenty miles so the truckers who came in from Newark didn't know its final destination. Mitch asked him how long he had been with Joseph. Dom told him not that long; he had recently been discharged from the army and his father had pulled in a marker with Joseph, asking him to find a job for Dom. Joseph liked Dom and gave him a job guarding his back.

"Why?" asked Mark.

"I guess he figured that after two tours in Bosnia Herzegovina, I was good enough to cover his six," said Dom.

"So, when we were in the restaurant, were you supposed to shoot me before I shot him?"

"Something like that, except Jonathan showed up and I had to shoot him."

"Didn't you read the autopsy, Dom? Either of our bullets could have killed him."

"Copy that."

"Army?" asked Mitch, to break the tension.

"Ranger, sniper," said Dom.

"Welcome aboard, soldier," said Mitch.

Dom suddenly realized that to play in the big leagues with this team, you had to be ready: when the team was down by three, the bases were loaded, it was the last of the ninth, and you were up at bat with a full count; if you didn't hit the last pitch up and out over the center field wall for a home run, you got traded to a farm team in Moose Jaw, Saskatchewan. He was impressed.

"So where's the FBI?" he asked.

Mitch pointed at the chain-link fence behind the house. "There and there, in the shrubbery."

"Why not inside the house?" asked Dom.

"We couldn't come up with a way to smuggle them into the house during the morning because we figured it could be under surveillance. For the same reason, we couldn't post them on the back porch. It would have been great if the bad guys had come up behind them and cold cocked them in their rockers. So Frank and Peter played a chilly game of tennis at the club behind the fence and then snuck around through the only gate into the shrubbery. They're actually pretty good; we've worked with them before."

"Although Peter did whip Frank's ass," added Mark. "He's played this game before."

"He's ranked professionally," said Mitch.

"What do we do now?" asked Dom.

"We sit and wait, and once in a while one of us goes into that empty house with a toolbox, pretending to fix a broken air conditioner that doesn't exist."

Dom sighed and picked up the toolbox. "I guess it'll be my turn next."

They watched as a white truck slowly turned the corner.

"Oops," said Mark, "Who's this?"

"The caterers," said Mitch. "We were told to expect them."

They watched as a cart was loaded and wheeled toward the house. They could almost smell the food from there.

"Wait a minute!" exclaimed Dom. "Weren't the caterers supposed to be two men?"

"Yes!" said Mitch, and in a second he was on his cell phone to the caterers. After a frustrating delay, he yelled "It's going down. Call Frank!"

But Mark had already done that and Frank and Peter were moving.

"Is it time to go now?" asked Dom.

But he was talking to an empty truck—Mitch and Mark were already gone.

The doorbell rang and Gladys hastened to answer. In came Boris and Natasha with the turkey dinner, which they began to serve. There was a huge turkey on a tray, as well as containers filled with vegetables and gravy, mashed potatoes, two pies, and even cornbread stuffing in a cast iron pan. Em sniffed; she was old-school and liked the stuffing inside the bird, but she knew modern chefs liked to make it separately. It was easier to prepare large quantities that way. In her mind, you were sacrificing quality for quantity.

Boris had never carved a turkey and clearly had no idea how to go about it. In fact, he couldn't even hold the carving knife and fork. Henry rose and prepared to take over when Boris suddenly handed the knife to Natasha. All attention shifted to her as it became obvious to everyone that she didn't have a clue either. Then Irving noticed her white coat was too large for her and the name embroidered on it in red was "Fred." He started to point when she brandished the carving knife and shouted, "Der'mo! No one move!"

The tableau froze—until Irving "Frisbeed" an empty dinner plate at Natasha—hitting her on the forehead and opening a sizeable cut that began to bleed profusely, dripping into her left eye. Henry seized the moment to drive his elbow into Boris's stomach, halting him in his tracks. Then Henry hit him again and this time Boris turned his attention to the annoying old man.

Natasha wiped at her eye and came at Irving with the knife, screaming profanity in Russian. Boris yelled at her to leave DJ alone, so she shifted her attention to Em.

Meanwhile, Irving had grabbed the wooden carving platter from under the turkey and managed to get it in front of Em like a shield, so when Natasha's knife came at her it stuck harmlessly. Then Irving hit Natasha twice more with the board and she collapsed to the floor.

"Mother always taught me to be courteous toward women, but there are exceptions to every rule," he said.

On the other side of the huge dining room table, Henry was not faring nearly as well. He was giving twenty kilos and forty—no make that almost fifty years—away to Boris, but he was quick and figured all he had to do was slow Boris down a little until help arrived. And it did come, in the form of Frank, who came through the back door like an express train, with Peter right behind him.

Unfortunately, Gladys chose that moment to get into the fight. She grabbed the turkey by a drumstick, wound up, and hurled it at Boris, like she was throwing a fastball. He ducked and it missed him, but it did a slow, midair somersault, and Frank wound up wearing it like a helmet. He went down on top of Peter in a welter of arms and legs. They were out of the fight until they could get untangled.

Boris had Henry pinned against the wall and was about to swing his fist in a blow with all of his one hundred kilos behind it; he smiled as he started to swing. But Em came to the rescue. She held the cast iron cornbread pan in both hands and swung it like she was going to hit a home run, putting all of her 102 and a half pounds behind her swing. Boris hit it dead center, making a sound that would be remembered by everyone in the room. He stood there in a daze, looking down at his hand, which was now hanging limply from his broken wrist.

Em then hit him with a glancing blow over the head, making his knees buckle. That brought his head down to where Em could do a proper job on it.

"Try to hit my husband," she said, as she bashed Boris again. Henry pulled her away before she could do any more harm.

The fight was over, and so was dinner, the remnants of which were scattered around the room.

"Can someone get Frank off me?" asked Peter.

"Can someone get this damned turkey off my head?" asked Frank from inside the turkey.

Henry gave Frank a hand up and reached down for Peter, who none too gently yanked the turkey from Frank's head.

"You're all under arrest!" shouted Frank.

Henry and Em pulled out their badges, reminding Frank who everyone was.

Mitch and Mark had arrived on the scene in time to see the last of the punches. "Nice job," Mitch said to Henry, Em, and Irving. "Gladys, as soon as the dust settles, we'll take you down to where the real DJ lives and give you a turkey dinner you will never forget," promised Mitch.

"I think I just had one," she answered, looking around her ruined dining room.

That brought a laugh from everyone except Frank—he turned to look at her and held her gaze. Boris and Natasha were slowly coming to. Frank handcuffed them together, since Boris's hand was broken, and called an ambulance.

Boris and Natasha were eventually convicted of all sorts of felonies, misdemeanors, and cybercrimes. The judge stipulated that during their ten-year incarceration, under no circumstances were either of them allowed access to a personal computer or the Internet.

Appeal was denied, and they both said they'd have preferred a lethal injection.

Chapter 18

Oh, Happy Holidays!

I**T WAS 8 P.M. THAT** night and Gladys sat down to pour herself a stiff drink. The cleanup crew had come and gone, and the only two people left in the home were Gladys and, of all people, Irving, who had decided to stay and chat with Gladys for a while. He already had his drink in hand and was nodding appreciatively at the taste of the fine Scotch over ice.

"So, young man," said Gladys, "what exactly do you do?"

"I'm a computer tech—a geek—I guess you could say."

Gladys nodded as if she knew exactly what he was talking about.

"Is that what my son is, too?"

"Yup," nodded Irving, not particularly wanting to get into the details of what DJ actually did—and had done!

"Well, I guess that's what you young geniuses do these days. I could never figure DJ out." She sighed for a minute and then brightened up. "I guess someone in your company discovered what he was good for and put him to work at it. That makes me happy."

Irving nodded, pleased that the question-and-answer period was over so quickly.

Em and Henry were driving north on the Thruway; they'd left Westbush at about 6 p.m. and were chatting happily about the day's adventure.

"I have to hand it to you, girl," said Henry, "just when I think I know everything there is to know about you, you show me some new stuff!"

Em laughed her best wicked laugh. "Yeah, Jared asks us, in all good faith, to come down to Westbush to play grandma and gramps to DJ and his mom. Guess we showed them a thing or two, didn't we, Henry?"

"We sure did, little lady, we sure as hell did. And it was fun, too, wasn't it?"

"I hate to ask you this, Henry," added Em, "but do you possibly have some aching muscles? I know I do."

Henry harrumphed, and since Em couldn't tell from that what was on his Henry's mind, she continued. "I saw a sign a mile or two back for a lovely little motel advertising rooms with Jacuzzis. How would you like to stop at one of those for the night? We're not in any big hurry to get back to the B&B, are we?" hinted Em.

Henry already had his turn signal on as the next exit sign came into view.

Half an hour later, as they settled their tired bodies into the warm, jetted bathtub, Em grinned, and Henry let out a sigh of relief.

"Now this is the *life*," they said almost in unison, as they were prone to do after so many years together. Em had tossed a tiny container of bubble bath into the water, and soon they were up to their necks in foam, tossing bits of suds back and forth.

"I can't get over you and that skillet," said Henry. For a little gal, you've got a pretty strong arm."

"You're no slouch yourself," quipped Em, "no slouch at all!"

Every once in a while, Em would add more hot water, and before they knew it, they were getting tired.

"You sleepy, Em?" asked Henry.

"Yup," she answered, "but not *that* sleepy that we couldn't make a little time for fun."

With a bit of effort, Henry stood up, bubbles clinging to his bare backside, and sent a large, fluffy towel flying in Em's direction.

———— ❧ ————

Ellen was back at their apartment in DC, missing Irving with a pain that was almost physical. She wasn't used to being away from him, and she was pushing herself to keep from falling into a funk. Nor was she in any kind of a holiday mood. She hadn't felt like shopping or going to parties or any of the fun things the season was known for. Instead, she was looking around their little apartment, which had been Irving's bachelor pad, thinking she'd have to pack up their belongings and get ready for their move to Vegas—scheduled for right after the New Year. Karen was getting housing ready, and Ellen hoped the change of scene would do her some good. She was definitely down in the dumps. Tomorrow she would call the office and ask Melanie to send over some boxes so she could pack. Then she slumped on the bed, got herself a container of yogurt to settle her stomach, and turned on the television. It was going to be a long night.

———— ❧ ————

Jared and Dee were in DC, having flown in from New York the previous evening. By the time Dee came awake, she realized how late in the morning it already was. She could hear Jared's voice coming from the communications room, so she slipped out of bed, put a robe on, and wandered in to say good morning. He held up one finger, letting her know he needed a minute to finish the call he was on.

"Morning, my love, how are you doing today?"

Jared stroked her back, and said softly, "I thought I'd let you rest. You were sleeping so soundly when I got up, I didn't have the heart to wake you."

"What are you working on, sweetie?" she asked.

"Wrapping up a lot of year-end details," came the reply. "There's so much to keep track of, and I can't let anything slip through the cracks. If I did, that would potentially put people in danger. I'll be going into the office in a little while."

Dee nodded. "So how did the operation in New Jersey go yesterday? Did they get the bad guys? Or the bad guy and girl?"

"Turns out it really was a man and a woman. We did get them, but it wasn't our usually smooth operation. My team doesn't normally have a 'miss' of this magnitude, but we were a day late for their arrival in the US, plus we didn't have enough information to make a positive ID as they came through customs and immigration. I think we also left too much to chance. Seems we have identified a weakness in our system that needs to be rectified. I've asked one of my security people to look into it and to prepare an updated training course."

"Good idea," said Dee. "After all, what good is a 'miss' if we don't learn from it? Would you like another cup of coffee, or are you ready for breakfast?"

Also in Washington, Melanie debriefed the few people on her team who had actually managed to get flights out of Newark the night before. At the moment, only Mitch and Mark were in the office.

"Let me get this straight, Mitch," Melanie said to her husband, "if I read the report correctly, the two of you actually arrived at the 'scene of the crime,' as it were, *after* it ended?"

Mitch let out a huge sigh. "It wasn't so much that we were *late*," he said, "but that it all went down rather quickly."

"Lessons learned?" she snapped back.

"Yes, ma'am," he said to his wife, "we are rewriting a number of procedures as we speak. First, and our biggest error, is that we positioned ourselves—meaning our service truck—too far away from the action, as it were."

"Relax," said Melanie. "I think under normal surveillance conditions, the truck and its occupants were positioned correctly. You lost precious time checking on the caterers by phone, especially having to wait so long for someone to give you the description of the two delivery people. Can you see how every second counts?"

"I won't let it happen again," said Mitch, who looked like he was starting to relax.

Then Melanie said what was really on her mind. "When Jared decides to formally debrief me, I will have some explaining to do myself, so don't feel so bad, okay? You and Mark both did a very good job, and I'm sure if Em and Henry *hadn't* been there, and you were the only 'intervening party,' Boris and Natasha would still have ended up under arrest. Boris might even have survived without the broken wrist." Then she let out an uncharacteristic chuckle.

"What I didn't expect—what you didn't think about and what none of us could have predicted—is what Em and Henry did in that short space of time. Time and again we underestimate them. Those two are really something else!"

Melanie watched as Mitch and Mark exchanged glances. They looked relieved, and she half expected to hear them laughing out loud as soon as they'd closed her door.

It was 5:45 p.m. and Karen sat waiting for Mark at Las Brasas Restaurant, their hangout near the office. They had dinner reservations for 6 p.m., and Karen arrived early, so she took a seat at the bar and ordered a cosmopolitan. It had been a rough day and she needed a little time to unwind; the extra minutes gave her time to get out of "office mode" and relax.

But before her drink arrived, she felt—rather than saw—someone take the chair to her left. "Hi there, pretty lady, can I buy you a drink?"

Uh oh, Karen recognized the voice. It was Dom, and he was putting on the full measure of "bar charm." What Dom didn't know was that this kind of behavior was at the top of Karen's hate list. And he was about to make it much worse. When Karen didn't answer right away, he upped the ante. "Watsamatter, Karen? You always this uptight? I know a few good ways to relax you, if you know what I mean..."

Dom never saw the punch coming, and he didn't stick around for long either. Wiping his nose with the back of his sleeve, he headed for the exit, nearly bumping into Mark as he pushed the door open.

Mark found Karen at the bar, calmly sipping her drink. "Wasn't that Dom? Wonder why he was in such a hurry..."

Karen never said a word. But later that night, after a romantic dinner, she took five minutes out of her beauty routine to place a short call to Melanie. She knew Melanie would understand.

And she did.

Chapter 19

Traded to the Farm Team

THE NEXT MORNING MELANIE CALLED Dom into her office. His nose was still tender and swollen, and he knew what this meeting had to be about. He had his excuses ready and his resignation letter in hand.

Melanie glared at him. "Sit down and don't say a word."

Dom looked at her and figured he could save face by resigning before he was fired.

"We are a family! We spar with each other to maintain our fitness to deal with our jobs. But we don't try to hurt each other for spite. Karen and Mark are a couple as are Ellen and Irving and Mitch and I. Those relationships are off-limits. Do I make myself *clear*?"

"Uh, okay," was all he could stammer.

"All right, put the stupid resignation letter back in your pocket and listen up for your next assignment. I spend a lot of time looking for talent like yours and when I find it, I'm not going to waste it. I understand you have a desire to visit Moose Jaw, Saskatchewan, so I'm giving you the opportunity to do just that."

Oh shit! He thought, I've been traded to the farm team. How the hell did she know what I said?

"Be careful what you wish for," she said with an evil smile, "you might just get it. There's a large company in Moose Jaw that makes shale oil distillation equipment. There's also a start-up company that has a cheaper, better process. Jared has

126

been asked to help with it and has also invested in the startup. However, they seem to be having production problems. There is at least one rifleman and maybe more who are shooting holes in the tanks on the exterior of their building, shutting down production for at least a week each time it happens. The tanks contain hazardous materials that cannot be moved indoors under Canadian environmental regulations. The local mounted police can't locate the snipers and have asked for our support. Are you up for it?"

"Yes!" was all he said, thinking he had fallen into a shit pool and come up smelling like a rose. "Do I get to carry?"

"Of course you do. Choose your own rifle from our armory. You have two days to sight it in and then you're off to the frozen north. We'll ship it and it will be ready for you when you get there. Pack your long johns and your parka; it's December, remember." She smiled sweetly.

"Roger that!" he said. "And thank you for the second chance."

"Get this right, or I'll leave you up there," she said, "and you'll walk home. Now get out of here."

Dom strolled up to Mitch and Mark at the outdoor shooting range, where they were having a little practice. They were shooting at twenty-five meters and both had all five shots inside the nine ring for the last five targets. Dom showed them the target he held: it had five holes that you could cover with a coffee cup.

"Needs some work," said Mark, still not Dom's best friend. Mitch smiled.

"Fifteen hundred meters," said Dom. "Wind was a little fluky."

"All right," said Mark, after taking a deep breath and extending his hand.

"So you got the Moose Jaw job?" asked Mitch.

"Better you than us!" laughed Mark.

Better than a vet with no job and homeless on the street, thought Dom, reminding himself about where part of his next paycheck would go.

Dom checked into the Moose Jaw Inn and headed downtown looking for a place to get some Intel—and, of course, a beer.

The third bar he saw was well lit and the parking lot was full so he decided this was the one. It was crowded and friendly with the kind of camaraderie that exists among those who make their living in adverse environments. He found a place at the bar and ordered a Labatt. The man on his left looked him up and down and said, "New here, ay?"

"In here for a consulting job. Is it always this ball-freezing cold?"

"Hell, it's just beginnin' to get cold, ay? Wait 'til February? Where're you from, ay?"

"Bahstin," said Dom, dragging out the accent. "It's cold out theyah, but nothin' like theas."

"So what brings you up to this godforsaken place, ay?"

"Working for a small company that needs some help," said Dom, suppressing his accent as much as possible. "Makes some sort of shale oil processing equipment and they have a technical problem. If I told you any more, I'd have to shoot you."

"Wouldn't have to. I know who and what you're talking about. I drive the UPS truck, so if you want to know what's going on, talk to me, ay." It seemed like he ended every sentence with a rising inflection and "ay," which made it a question and sounded like "nay" without the "n."

Dom gave him a curious look.

"It's David and Goliath. Juno Shale has been here forever, and this little company, Yukon, starts up out of nowhere. Has some new tech or hardware that's eating Juno's lunch. So Juno tries to enforce an expired patent to stop them, but this big law firm from New York shows up and blocks it with a countersuit. Juno backed down, can you believe it?"

I wonder who did it, thought Dom, knowing the answer, of course.

"Then Juno tried to do some sort of crazy financial thing that was supposed to freeze Yukon's credit lines and put them out of business. But suddenly there was another investor guaranteeing new lines so they could stay open."

Dom smiled as it became clear why he was here.

"It's mystified all of us up here. Now they are up against a deadline to ship product but someone is sabotaging their plant by firing bullets at it. Some employees won't even show up for work anymore. But it's not at the employees, it's at some tanks out back they can't bring inside because of CSA regulations. Each time they get hit it costs them a week to get back up and running, and soon they'll run out of time, ay?"

"So can't the Mounties put a stop to it?" asked Dom.

"Because the land behind the plant is wide open and flat land with a few scraggly trees. Acres and acres of it. Great place to snowmobile on weekends—lots of tracks—fun place. But during the week everyone's at work and it's a huge area to patrol. No way the Mounties can cover it; all four that are assigned to this region," he said, smiling. "They do the best they can, but they have to patrol the town now and again, do you see, ay?"

Dom changed direction. "I thought there would be a lot more snow up here. Where do you hide it?"

That brought a laugh. "Oh, we have enough of it when it snows. But then the wind blows it all into Manitoba. Good riddance, I say."

Dom bought him another beer and headed for the door.

"Early morning tomorrow at the factory. Travelling is such a bitch, ay?"

His newfound friend laughed. "You're starting to sound like one of us, ay?"

"Give me another week, ay?" said Dom.

Dom showed up at the local Mountie's office the next morning to make sure his rifle had arrived. The sergeant was impeccably dressed in his red uniform and correct and formal in his demeanor, but Dom could see that he was not happy about having a sniper rifle in his jurisdiction in Canada. Of course, Dom also knew there were bad feelings because he had been sent to unravel the tank shootings, a case the Mounties hadn't been able to solve. The sergeant produced the weapon and handed it to Dom, who cleared it, checked it, and handed it back to him.

"May I have your name and rank?" asked the sergeant.

"First lieutenant, retired. Call me Dom. Now, how many people know this came in?"

"No one has seen it but me," said the sergeant. "I personally accepted it, signed for it, and unwrapped it."

"Your name is?"

"Preston," came the flat response.

"Good, let's keep it that way for now," said Dom, looking deep into the sergeant's eyes.

"Yes, sir!" the sergeant replied.

Dom wondered if he'd chosen the right career. Here he was ankle deep in snow and chopped-off wheat or corn stalks and freezing his ass off in the middle of a huge field—with little or no cover as far as he could see. He was looking for a sniper—great job!

Okay, get professional, and don't think about your freezing ass.

He started sighting on the tanks that had been hit. That was easy, because there were orange tarps over them to protect the men repairing them.

Hmmm, thought Dom, if I wanted to hit those tanks, what would be my line of fire? The sergeant had told him it was the 5.56×45 mm NATO cartridge with a supersonic, flat trajectory, easily fired from where Dom stood and only requiring one bullet to do the job every time. *So that meant the guy was good: at least as good as I am.*

He spent the next hour wandering up and down the snowmobile tracks. Although any footprints had been erased by the wind, it was obvious where they had stopped and compressed the snow. Most of the prints were in a specific spot. Dom looked down the monocular he was carrying and saw the tanks. Field and spread of fire about ten degrees. He looked behind him. There were a couple of scraggly trees and the same 'no cover' ground that he was looking at.

"Oh well, make do! Improvise! Etc.!" he recited. Screw this, he thought. At least he'd found out most of the shots were made during the late morning, when the sun would be behind the shooter.

He showed up at the Mountie station the next morning and Sergeant Preston was there, impeccably dressed.

"May I have my rifle?" Dom asked courteously. Forms were passed forward for him to sign.

"Thank you," he said.

"Always glad to assist our southern neighbors." Sergeant Preston excused himself and went to retrieve the weapon.

"If you are unsuccessful in your endeavors today, please return it to our custody when you are done," he said evenly. "We'll keep it for you until tomorrow."

Dom collected his rifle and laid a hand-held radio on the sergeant's desk.

"Anything else I can do for you?" asked Preston.

"Keep listening to the radio, and if I call, be prepared to come and make an arrest."

"That's not standard issue," said Preston.

"True," said Dom, "but whoever is doing this has been listening in on your communication links and this one is secure—very secure."

Preston gave him a wry look and picked up the radio gingerly.

"Incidentally, we've discovered their frequencies and I will be monitoring them while I'm out on the tundra."

"And where, exactly, will that be?"

"About one thousand meters north of this point," said Dom, pointing at the map on the wall.

"Isn't that a little far?" asked Preston.

Dom lifted the rifle and looked at him as one professional to another. That said it all.

Preston saluted him and Dom took the weapon and headed out the door.

From 10:00 to 14:00 he froze his ass off once again out in the field. Then he had to return the rifle to Sergeant Preston, who with a straight face asked him when he would like to collect it again. Dom returned his mock salute. "Same time, same station."

Dom needed sustenance, so after emailing his report to Melanie and a taking short nap, he headed back to his favorite watering hole. Sure enough, his UPS friend was there and made room for him at the bar.

"No, the part they needed for the tank was held up in customs, ay? Won't be in until late tonight. I get double time to pick it up and deliver it. Must be quite important. I'm getting double time for it!"

Great, another day freezing my ass off, ay? Oh, shit! I'm starting to sound like a native. Damn! Ay?

"My I have my rifle?" asked Dom, for the second day in a row.

"Of course," said Sargent Preston, nodding as much as his starched collar would allow. Then he went to get it.

"Wonder if he ever drove a dog sled?" mused Dom, as he noticed a trophy on the wall. "Third in the 2006 Iditarod."

Oh, shit! thought Dom. This guy is the real deal.

The slightly built Frenchman brought his snow machine to a stop where he had been twice before. It was in the middle of the week and all of the real folk were working, so he was all alone.

The Frenchman shouldered his Mauser rifle and looked down range. It was an easy shot, even at 1200 meters, and he thought that he didn't even need a scope. All he had to do was dent the one remaining tank and the company would be out of business for at least another week, if not forever. He hoped this wouldn't be the case because he was getting rich doing this. He jacked a cartridge into the gun, sighted carefully, and squeezed the trigger. The shot sounded like a whip crack when the gun went off and he counted silently to himself waiting for impact. He saw it through the scope before he heard it: a dimple appeared on the side of the tank! A little high and to the right, but the job was done. He kept counting, waiting for the echo. It came and was surprisingly loud. It rang in his ears. He shook his head to clear them.

The job was done and he turned back to his snow machine; except now it wouldn't start. It wouldn't even crank over. Then he looked down and saw the hole in the side of the crankcase. Realization struck him like a hammer blow. Where had *that* come from? Why hadn't he heard it? He looked around wildly, but all he could see were scrub stalks and snow. There had to be someone out there, but where?

He decided to hike out and turned back down the path, but a

spurt of snow in front of him stopped him cold. Subconsciously, he started counting the seconds. Two and a half seconds later he heard the sound of the shot. He did the math in his head. *Sacre merde! 1400 meters!* He grabbed his rifle and looked around again. A man was standing with a rifle pointed at him. It was too late—he didn't have a chance and he knew it. He slowly put his gun down in the snow and sat on his snow machine to wait. It didn't take long; he heard the high-powered truck coming up the road. It was red, with the Royal Canadian Mounted Police logo emblazoned on the side. Sergeant Preston got out. "I arrest you in the name of the Queen," he said. The Frenchman held out his hands.

When he looked up, the man with the rifle was gone.

Dom laid the rifle down on the sergeant's desk. "I've been instructed to leave it here and to tell you to use it at your own discretion," he said.

"I thank you in the Queen's name," Preston said formally, and then leaned forward. "Those were two exceptionally long shots, right on spot to keep him there."

"Two? How did you know?"

"The snow melted around where you ejected the first round, which you picked up. You were also clever, walking backward up to the shooting point. However, when you came back, there were slight overlaps in the footprints."

Dom looked at him with new respect.

"One thing puzzles me," continued Preston. "The shot that disabled the snow machine. May I ask how you did it without alerting Francoise?"

"The only cover was 1400 meters away," said Dom. "I waited until I saw his bullet hit the tank. I knew the sound would take three and a half seconds to get back to him. My bullet would take one and a half seconds to hit his engine. So I counted to two and fired. He didn't even know what happened. By the way, I called you before he took the shot; I didn't want to have to shoot him because he might give you some information about who was behind this."

Preston gave him a long, hard look and then shook his head. "If you ever want a job up here in God's country, give me a call," he finally said. "You are quite correct—he has been most cooperative since we explained his options to him." He smiled thinly. "Perhaps I exaggerated the penalties slightly, but he seemed to understand. Unfortunately, some of the criminals do not reside in Canada."

"That's above my pay grade," said Dom, "but I think the people I work for will have some ways to deal with them." They shook hands and Dom left, wondering if he would ever have to drive a dog sled.

Shortly thereafter the sergeant received a phone call.

Preston," he answered.

"Is the situation resolved?" asked Jared.

"Yes, but as I explained to your employee, we are not able to reach out to the people who are responsible."

"Leave it to me. We do have the means to make their investments turn sour, their businesses fail, and, in general, make them unhappy."

"Thank you," said Preston. "If I can be of any assistance in the future, I will be happy to oblige you." He rang off and wondered if what had happened in the past week was real or fantasy.

Dom was sitting in the bar in Moose Jaw with his newfound friends when his cell phone rang. It was Melanie. "Good job,

Dom. There's a first-class ticket home waiting for you at the airport." He laid a hundred Canadian on the bar, shook hands all around, and said, "Gotta go."

Chapter 20

Where Did the Year Go?

THE COCKTAIL PARTY WAS IN full swing. Dee looked lovely in a black cocktail dress, and Jared was elegant in his tux. "Galleria D" was lit up like a movie set, and the rooms were filled with the city's most beautiful people. Jared had flown his mother and Dee's sister, Leah, in from Washington, DC, but the main focus was on the clients Dee had worked so hard to cultivate more than four years ago. Almost everyone she invited had accepted her invitation, and they greeted her with such warmth that she was overwhelmed with happiness and pride.

The gallery had a new coat of paint in a shade of cream specially designed to bring out the warmth of the paintings. New lighting had also been installed. More than a dozen emerging artists were being showcased, and there was something for everyone, from the lovers of primitives to the modernists. All were represented, and there were bios and photos of the artists alongside each work. No detail had been overlooked.

Dee had chosen "Around the World" as her theme for the opening. There were colorful, fragrant floral arrangements in each room. The catering was first-class, with the wine and food selected to match the regions of the world from which the paintings originated. Dee had brought her vision to work in record time, and no one had ever doubted she would. She was back!

…Yet across the street, one person was following the evening's activities from the shadows.

———————⁓⁓⁓⁓⁓⁓———————

Karen took a red-eye back from Las Vegas, choosing to fly through Chicago instead of Dallas-Fort Worth. It turned out to be a bad decision, since she was routed to Newark instead of Washington, DC due to bad weather conditions. She had planned to visit Melanie at home and to give her an update on how the work in Vegas was progressing. Instead, she called her from Chicago, and Melanie told her to check into the Westbush Inn and help Mark with a routine surveillance.

This Las Vegas job has more tentacles than an octopus, Karen thought, as her plane descended into Newark. *Every time I think I get my hands around it, more things crop up. I need to stop having meetings with the security team and wrap up the project scope and parameters. If I don't, in five years we will still be ramping up.* She could, however, point to certain accomplishments. A well-organized office and two apartments—hers and another for Ellen and Irving—were ready for occupancy after the first of the year, which, she realized, was only a few days away. Where had the year gone?

As the plane's engine hum changed pitch, she thought back over the year. She'd put away a tidy sum for herself that night in Las Vegas when they brought Steve Milan down at roulette. Jared's generosity had given her a sense of security. She was happy for Jared; he had gone from being alone—and seemingly a loner—to a man with a lovely lady by his side, and they were engaged. Melanie had begun the year newly wed to Mitch and was now preparing for motherhood. The business had grown by leaps and bounds. How many security people had Mitch and Mark trained this year? Thirty? Forty? And then DJ came on board. What a crazy fluke that was! But what a nice addition to the balance sheet. Jared had made some powerful bankers very happy.

And Mark! Karen still wasn't sure of Mark. She needed to spend more time with him, away from work, to find out what he was like as a person and particularly as a potential mate. When he was working, he was so serious, but she needed some playtime, maybe even a short vacation with him, to see if they could be compatible on a long-term basis. That was the one problem she saw with the kind of work they all did. It was high stress, and not easy to come down off the "high" when you wanted to relax. But, she had seen how both Jared and Mitch had softened with loving women in their lives, and she wondered if it could be the same for Mark. Only time would tell, but when would they find the time? She hoped her unplanned stay in Westbush would give her a chance to get to know him better.

Em had wanted to bring Henry to New York City to attend the gallery opening, but it was the week between Christmas and New Year's, and Green Haven was filled to overflowing. Extra help had been brought in because most of their regulars had also become friends and wanted to spend time with the two of them. It had also become a special week because of their love of baking and decorating. The best times were the chilly nights when they lit a fire in the huge fireplace and brought out the eggnog, celebrating with their guests. Em's only wish was that Dee and Jared could have been there with them, but she understood why they couldn't.

Meanwhile, back in Washington DC, Melanie was struggling through the holidays in her own way. Eight months along, she had the mental energy to keep up her schedule, but her growing

girth made it hard for her to get in and out of her Mazda Miata.
So, when Mitch was in town he would chauffer her in one of the
company sedans; her alternative was to work from home, which
was what she was doing for Christmas week. In fact, the entire
office was on a reduced work schedule, which was fine with her.

DJ was visiting his mother in Westbush for a few days.
Melanie realized it was a calculated risk to let him out of her
sight, because she knew there was still a price on his head, but
she wanted him to have a Christmas vacation. So, like it or not,
she kept up her routine surveillance. In fact, Mark had an easy
time of it, because DJ hadn't gone very far. Every day he ate
his way across the town's six-block long Main Street. So now
Melanie had Mark, joined by Karen, to keep watch as DJ went to
Panera's for breakfast, to Chipotle Grill for lunch, to Starbucks
for his afternoon coffee fix, and to Mario's for his dinner pizza.
Mark called Melanie every once in a while to let her know that,
as far as he could tell, no one else seemed to be tailing DJ.

It was, however, too soon to make that call.

Dom had been apartment hunting in DC, since he'd already
closed up the place he'd rented in Boston. He'd put almost
everything he owned—which wasn't much—into one of those
storage containers you could ship down on the back of a truck.
That is, if he could find someplace to live. He hadn't counted on
Washington prices when he signed the contract with Melanie.
Every place he could afford had something wrong with it. He
nixed it if there were too many kids around or if they allowed
dogs or even if he didn't like the way the cars were parked in
the lot.

He wanted a homey place like the one he had in the north
end of Boston, near the neighborhood bar, in the back of an
alley, with a landlady who told him the gossip from the block

when he came home at night. DC was all glitz and glass or fern and brick, he decided, which wasn't his style.

So, until he could find a place in DC, he hung out in Boston over the Christmas holidays, drinking with old friends. His meager possessions were already on their way to Washington, so he finally decided to pack up the rest of his stuff and head south in time for the New Year.

In New York City, Bart was in his elegant office reviewing Protek's financials. Jared and his various companies had enjoyed a banner year. Even considering the sometimes heavy investments in assets, such as Melanie's vehicle fleet, and their travel expenses, including the corporate jet, they were still so profitable that Bart shook his head and had to admire Jared's creativity and expertise. They were making millions on ventures other CEOs hadn't even thought about—at least not on a scope as large as Jared's. And the trend line was out of sight.

Bart was pleased that he himself was a minor investor. Even his small share had made him more money this past year than his entire law firm. Talk about the tail wagging the dog! Bart lifted an imaginary glass and whispered, "Happy New Year—and many, many more like this one!"

Chapter 21

Karen's Romantic Interlude

KAREN AND MARK WATCHED FROM the diner across the street as DJ sauntered into Panera for breakfast. Sitting in the front booth, she smiled at Mark, genuinely happy to see him again. Sometimes she thought she was getting closer to admitting her feelings, but she was never sure how well this would be received. So she just let her mind wander for a few moments. That turned out to be a mistake.

"How long has DJ been in there?" Mark finally asked.

"About twenty minutes," Karen said, checking her watch.

"That long to get a Danish and a Coke?"

They looked at each other and exploded into action: across the street and into the store, but by this time DJ was nowhere in sight.

Karen pushed to the front of the line, which didn't make her any friends.

"There was a scruffy kid in here with a sweatshirt and sneakers; where did he go?" she shouted.

The girl behind the counter quickly answered her. "He was here, bought a glazed donut and a Coke. And sat over there," she said pointing. "Then two men came in from the back and sat at his table. They talked to him for a minute and then they left through the rear entrance."

By the time she'd finished her answer, Karen was gone.

Karen already had the Jeep Cherokee started and in gear when Mark jumped into the passenger side. She remembered how DJ always liked to ride in the back with the wind in his hair like some sheepdog with his nose out the window, but the truth was no one would ever let him drive because he was a terrible driver, a danger to himself, to those who rode with him, and to any other innocent person on the road. Up to this point he had been easy to guard. Now he was gone!

"Is his tracker on?" asked Karen from behind the wheel.

"Yes, in a bright moment, I turned it on."

"Pity we both didn't have more bright moments," said Karen, acidly. "How far ahead of us is he?"

"Getting close to max range; we'd better hustle."

As Karen drove down the New Jersey Turnpike, Mark got on the speaker phone to Melanie. After he explained that they'd lost DJ and listened to a tense three-minute lecture, he asked, "What backup can you give us?"

"I'll see what I can do," came the icy reply, and then the line clicked dead.

Karen and Mark shared a brief glance—she knew they were in deep trouble and on their own until Melanie could get them some backup.

She made time by breaking several speed limits, weaving in and out of traffic to close the distance until Mark said, "Oops, they're getting off at the next exit!" She cut through three lanes of traffic and made the exit ramp amid a chorus of angry horns.

The country road wasn't easy to follow and it eventually petered out into a snow-covered, rutted track. When the SUV they had been following stopped at a remote cabin in the middle of the woods, Karen stopped a short distance away, hoping that whomever they had been following wouldn't notice.

She was wrong.

Mark jumped out of the Jeep first and told her in no uncertain terms to stay in the car. She had a moment of *do what?* And then decided Mark was the best man for the job. While she didn't like it, she stood by the car cooling her jets, waiting for him to do whatever he had to do. Instinctively she knew Mark was the best in the business. They would get DJ back and paddle his ass! She smiled at the thought and wondered where it had come from. When she looked up again, Mark was nowhere in sight.

Meanwhile, back at the ranch, DJ was being forced to sit down in front of a computer. He grimaced as he looked at it. *Where in hell did they get this antique?* He was even more appalled when he tried the Internet connection. "I hope you don't expect me to do anything with this junk." He was amazed to hear that he was supposed to download everything about how he and his friends had scammed the scammers. "On this piece of crap?" he stammered. "Not a chance! Besides it's against the law!" he said, righteously.

His kidnapper lifted DJ's left hand and started to press a knife down on the middle knuckle. His intention was clear. DJ paled and found some inner strength. "That makes a lot of sense," he said, his voice dripping with sarcasm to mask his fear. "First of all, I faint at the slightest pain, and after you revive me, how do you expect me to type on this keyboard? I need all my fingers for that!"

His kidnapper appeared to think for a moment and then pocketed the knife. "We will torture your mother," he said. DJ paled further. "No, we will torture your cats to death, one by one!" At the horror of this being done to his beloved cats, DJ was ready to cave in.

Suddenly the man was spun violently around and the next thing DJ saw was his captor writhing in pain on the floor!

"All right, nitwit," came a familiar voice, "let's get out of here." It was Mark! He helped DJ to his feet and together they headed for the door. Unfortunately, it opened before they got there, and it was Karen who was now standing in the doorway. DJ smiled in recognition. Mark started to move, but a gun appeared next to her temple. He stopped as a second kidnapper shoved Karen roughly across the room at him. A moment later he caught her as gently as he could.

"I'm sorry," was all she could say.

"Shut up!" the other man hissed. "On the floor, hands behind your back!"

Mark gave him a vicious look and began to comply. He wasn't quite fast enough and Karen was pulled away and thrown to the floor. His hands were tied behind his back with plastic wire ties. He didn't say anything, but his eyes said it all. *This wasn't over yet.*

This was true because now the kidnapper on the floor was coming around. His partner pulled him to his feet and he looked around groggily. When he saw Mark, he roared, stood up, and started kicking him, first in the body and then in the face. Mark rolled with the kicks and managed to escape serious injury, but he knew what tomorrow morning would feel like—if he lived that long.

The second man pulled his partner off and told him they had work to do. They had a brief conversation in a language Mark didn't understand, so he looked on in stunned silence.

"Do what my friend here told you to do and we will let you and your friends go free," said the second kidnapper. "I hear that your friend faints at the first application of pain. However, you will comply with us to prevent his cats from being tortured. I propose a compromise." He lifted Karen up and put her left hand on the table. "All of you will comply with our requests or you will watch us cut off this young lady's fingers and listen to her scream in agony. I await your answer."

Mark watched as DJ sat back down at the computer. "You know with this junk computer it's going to take quite a while to do everything you want," he said.

He was handed a Post-it with an IP address.

"Just do it!" So he bent over the keyboard and logged in.

There they all sat waiting for DJ to perform an upload using a ridiculously slow connection while his captors did an equally slow boil.

"What's taking so long?" asked DJ's captor.

"I told you this computer was an antique and the connection was ridiculous."

"Well, hurry it up."

"Nothing I can do about it."

It was almost dark when the download was complete. A cell phone rang and the second captor answered it. He announced that the data checked out and had been used briefly. He clicked off, smiled, and said, "Well, now I don't need you anymore. Who shall I shoot first?"

Mark, still in serious pain and still tied up, had been watching from the floor. His surprise turned to happiness as DJ unwittingly created the perfect diversion: he turned and vomited on the computer's keyboard.

Mark had not been idle. In spite of his cuts and bruises, he did have some hope, one of which was the tiny cutter and knife he'd hidden in a small pocket in the back of his pants under his belt. He'd managed to get it out and was almost finished cutting through the plastic wire ties. His only thought now was about which of their two assailants he would hit first. The chances were slim he would get both of them, but he had to try. He figured he could take one of them down, take a bullet, and still injure the other one badly enough so the three of them could come out of this alive. He smiled to himself, *Optimist!*

For a moment DJ's vomiting had frozen the group in a tableau. Finally, the second man moved back toward the door, so he was standing next to his partner.

His hands finally free, Mark gathered his feet under him and launched himself off the floor, going for the man with the gun. But then the window behind him exploded and Mark missed, because the man simply wasn't there anymore. He subconsciously counted the shots: three in under two seconds.

The second shot hit Mark's target, sending the man up against the wall, a small red dot in the middle of his forehead. The third shot hit the second captor, taking out his right eye. Mark watched as he slid slowly to the floor. It was hard to process everything that had just happened.

Karen started to freak out, but somehow regained her control. Mark approached her carefully and cut the plastic ties that bound her hands.

In the quiet aftermath of the shooting, the three of them looked down at the two dead men and at each other. Not a word was spoken in those first few seconds.

Then the cabin door burst open again and Mark dove for the gun on the floor.

"Stop!" yelled Karen, before he could bring it up.

Dom stood in the doorway, a rifle in his hands. He looked at the two men on the floor, then at Mark and said to him, "Jesus, Mark, I thought you were better than this. Who beat the crap out of you?"

"They had to tie him up before they could do that," said Karen defensively. "He gave in to protect me."

Mark saw a look of understanding in Dom's eyes and smiled. "How the hell did you get here?" he asked.

"After the Moose Jaw job, and I thank you for that opportunity by the way, I went back to DC, but I had no place to stay for the holidays except an awful hotel. So I went back to Boston to get my stuff. And Melanie said I could have some time off. It was a good thing for all of us I wasn't stopped on the Mass Pike, because I had my dad's 30-06 Remington and a box of ammo in the back. Anyway, about the time I got to the New Jersey Turnpike, Melanie called and told me to turn on my tracker and get behind you as fast as I could – that you guys were in trouble. I couldn't locate you at first, but she zeroed me in, and because your bug was a lot stronger than DJ's, I was able to pick you up."

Mark smiled and nodded, rubbing his wrists at the same time.

Dom continued. "I missed the exit the first time and had to go to the next one and come back. Then I got lost twice trying to follow you. I nearly rear-ended your SUV coming around the last turn. I saw the lights of the cabin and headed here on foot. By that time, I was getting audio from your bugs. When I heard 'who shall I shoot first?' I put the rifle on a rock and took the shots. As it happened, the first bullet shattered the window and gave me clear field of fire. The bad guys were standing next to each other, so the second and third shots took them both out easily."

Karen looked at the two dead men on the floor and realized that could have been Mark and her if Dom hadn't shown up when he did. Her vision blurred, her knees went weak, and she almost fainted when she realized how close to death she had come. Mark and Dom caught her in time to keep her from falling to the floor. They held her up and looked into each other's eyes. Mark let her go first and extended his hand to Dom. "Thank you," he finally said. "You're a real pro."

"Two hundred yards?" said Dom with a smile. "Piece of cake."

"Let's get out of here."

"What do we do with these guys?" asked DJ.

Karen recovered quickly, and said, "We'll let the folks who sent them deal with them. But DJ, what about all the stuff you uploaded?"

DJ wiped his mouth and smiled. "When they try to use what I sent them, they will be very unhappy. In fact, they will have a few nasty surprises, not the least of which is that we can now trace back to *them* and squash them like cockroaches."

They looked at each other and headed for their SUVs.

"Don't you love that quiet week between Christmas and New Year's?" asked Karen sarcastically, as she helped Mark into the Jeep. Mark nodded, grimly.

Karen turned to Mark, a sly grin on her face. "What would you say to a few days far away from here, like an island in the Caribbean with a private beach? Where no one can find us? No cell service. No Internet!"

Mark groaned, and then a smile slowly spread across his bruised face. "If you can get Melanie to agree, I think I barely have enough energy left to carry your overnight bag."

"Is that all?" came the reply. "It's only fair to warn you I have a little more than that in mind."

Epilogue

THE BROAD EXPANSE OF LAWN had turned a pretty shade of emerald green; the sun had come out just in time for the start of the 2009 Memorial Day weekend. Melanie was the first outdoors that Saturday morning. Ellen watched as she emerged from the B&B carrying baby Evan on her hip, a blanket and a bottle in her other hand. She lowered him gently and he satisfied her motherly instincts by smiling and cooing at her with all the flirtatiousness a healthy four-month-old could muster.

Ellen followed her outside, carrying her own lawn blanket and the one cup of coffee she was allowed each day, given that she was now in her second trimester. She gave Melanie the special knowing look that passes from one mother to another as she sat down to join her.

"Did Dee and Jared arrive last night?" asked Ellen. "I didn't hear them come in. Our room's at the back this time, so I wouldn't have heard a car. And I didn't see them this morning at breakfast."

"I think their plane is due in around noon," answered Melanie. "They are going first to the construction site and plan to arrive here later in the afternoon. I hear the house is going to be gorgeous—a big farmhouse—and when you walk in you will feel like you have stepped into the previous century, much like Em and Henry have done here at Green Haven. Jared wants it to have views of the surrounding areas from every window."

"Dee's a lucky lady..." murmured Ellen, thinking things weren't so bad for any of them right now.

Melanie changed the subject. "Too bad Karen can't be here

this weekend. I told her to take the time off, but she wanted to complete the transfer of power. My maternity leave is over and she's writing wrap-up reports on everything that's happened since January. You know Karen; she wants it all in the files."

"Oh, she's great like that, isn't she?" said Ellen. "How are she and Mark doing? Anything you can talk about?"

"Funny thing about those two," mused Melanie. I guess I always thought Mark was a lot like my Mitch, but it seems he isn't. She wishes he'd talk more, you know, open up. She's crazy about him, but not every couple has a future. I've seen too many promising relationships go sour for less. I hope they stay together. I like them both a lot."

In the breakfast room, Mitch was quietly enjoying his second cup of coffee when Mark joined him. He reached for some of Em's homemade breakfast rolls with strawberry jam. As he looked up, he could see that Mark had something serious on his mind, so he waited for him to speak.

"Mitch, it's time I moved on. We were the best when we thought we were immortal."

Mitch nodded and began to answer.

"But now you are responsible for a wife and a son and that changes the balance."

Again Mitch began to speak, but Mark raised his hand. "Let me finish. You were always the one who made the instant decisions about tactics. We could read each other's minds. That's why we were the best. I was the aggressor. There's no one else I'd team up with now."

Mitch nodded and finally said, "What about Dom?" But he already knew that answer.

Mark almost choked on his coffee. "Dom? We're both aggressors! We'd wind up beating each other up more than the bad guys! No way *that's* going to work."

Mitch smiled. "What about Karen?" He thought he knew the answer to that too.

"She wants a husband like Melanie has," Mark said simply. "Someone who's strong enough to protect her and her family but is also vulnerable enough to talk about his innermost feelings and fears. I'm just *not* that guy."

"All right," Mitch finally said. "Melanie and I guessed this could be coming and we've already talked about it. She doesn't like it, but she's taking on some contracts that are only for solo agents."

Mark laughed. "Damn! Another Saskatchewan? My God, have I been traded to the farm team too?"

Mitch laughed, because the joke was now legendary around the company. "No, but who knows, maybe you can find a pretty young Inuit to keep your igloo warm during those long Arctic nights?"

They both laughed and the tension eased.

Then Mitch got serious again and continued. "You'll be on your own, but it doesn't mean your 'six' won't be covered. You know what happened when you and Karen were cornered."

"Dom?"

"No, Melanie, and she had two other options working. Dom just happened to be the nearest."

Mark looked thoughtful. "So I can stay with the company, go out in the field to risk my ass, and not have to go to feel-good meetings or train recruits?"

"Absolutely," Mitch said. "I've got that onerous job myself. But I want to know that if there's a really bad group we need to take down and they pull me off the bench and put me back in the game again, there's one man on the payroll I can trust to stand beside me."

Now it was Mark's turn to nod, and the two men stood and shook hands.

Dom chose that moment to saunter in. He picked up a coffee mug, filled it to the brim with black coffee, and sat down heavily. He ignored the silence and passed on the good mornings.

"Somethin' I've been meaning to tell you two," he opened. Two heads looked his way. "You know, I've still got friends back in Boston and they tell me things. Jared needs to know that Mary Rose is nosing around asking about Dee. Discreetly, but insistently. Jared might want to check that out." With that said, he moved on to the main salon, found the local paper, and sat down to read.

The Protek jet came to a stop in front of the small Columbia county terminal. Jared emerged first, followed by Dee, dressed from head to toe in Lily Pulitzer, a designer she'd found on a recent trip to Palm Beach where she viewed a show of local painters known as The Highwaymen. When she smiled at Jared her whole face lit up. The wind caught her hair as she descended the stairs. She'd let it grow longer, the way Jared liked, and she was the picture of health and happiness. She loved the way he looked at her, as though each time he saw her it was for the first time. She hoped that feeling would never go away, for either of them.

For a fleeting moment, her mind drifted to that night in New York City when Jared said he hoped someday he could finally toast to their future, knowing that she was safe and sound forever. She wondered about that for a moment and then let her thoughts turn to the weekend ahead.

THE END

We invite you to read a few pages of the sequel to **The Penny Scam**, entitled **Lady in Lace**, which will be coming out soon.

THE
Lady
in Lace

L. H. WILLIAMS

Prologue

MARY ROSE WOKE UP GROGGILY and rubbed her eyes. Her head ached and at first she couldn't remember where she was. Then she realized she was in her own bed in her own apartment.

But she wasn't alone.

She rolled over and looked at the swarthy man lying beside her. She didn't even remember his name – if she had ever known it.

She was disgusted with herself and everything she had become since Jonathan's death, as she now thought of what happened that fateful day.

She found her cell phone and dialed a number. It was answered immediately. "Yes?"

"Come here and remove this person from my apartment. Convince him he was never here and didn't spend the night. Convince him it would be better for if he forgot all about me. Make sure he understands completely."

"Yes, Miss Benefacio." And the line went dead.

She plodded into the bathroom and turned on the shower. She felt a little cleaner but the memories of what she had been doing in the last few months left a stench in her mind. She was in the kitchen making coffee when she heard the commotion in her bedroom. There was a surprised "Who the hell are you?" followed by the sound of blows, cries of pain and then the front door being slammed shut.

I have to stop this, she thought to herself.

It was an epiphany to her although she didn't even know what the word meant.

I need to see my Priest.

She dressed quickly, went to church and slipped into the confessional, where she was welcomed with open arms.

"Come, my child, God's forgiveness awaits you."

She sat quietly for a few moments while the Priest waited patiently.

Finally, she said, "I have sinned, Father, and there is no way I can stop myself. I know who and what I am. There is no forgiveness for me. This is my last confession."

Then she stood up and left the booth.

The Richest Man in New York

D EE STILL COULD NOT BELIEVE her ears! Klaus Vander Houten had just called and invited her to an "intimate cocktail party" to talk about art. She'd met him only once, when he'd stopped by the gallery a few years ago when she was still its manager. She knew him by reputation only – he was in his late seventies, single, somewhat of a recluse, and the owner of a magnificent art collection that included several European masters – all of it housed in a triplex penthouse located on the Upper East Side. She wondered idly who would be included in an "intimate cocktail party," never imagining what Klaus had in mind.

With Jared in Washington on business, Dee presented herself – alone – at the reception desk of Klaus's elegant old building and was asked to use the private elevator to the 20th floor. Klaus himself answered the door, which surprised her, and escorted her to a sweeping terrace where drinks and canapés had been laid out on a glass table. Her eyes took in the sweeping city view, and she thanked her host for inviting her, commenting on the gorgeous vista.

Much to her surprise, however, even though she had arrived almost half an hour late, she realized she was the first person to arrive, and she remarked on that, not sure whether she should feel embarrassed about being there so early.

Klaus led her to a patio chair, and seated her. "My Dear, I am so pleased you could join me for cocktails today. Perhaps you have not yet made the connection, but when I invited you to an 'intimate cocktail party' I meant just the two of us."

Dee's eyes opened wide as the implications of what Klaus said sunk in. Jared knew she was at a cocktail party, but – uncharacteristically – she had given him no further details, thinking there would be safety in numbers. Now there were no numbers. She was alone with a man she barely knew.

Klaus handed her a cocktail, and began softly. "First, my dear, I want to congratulate you on taking over the ownership of Galleria D, and also on your marriage. And, yes, I am aware that you recently married Jared Herreshoff, and you both have my best wishes. From what I have heard of him, he is a fine man – and you make a beautiful couple."

He continued. "I want you to know that I have watched your career from the beginning, ever since you came to New York straight from college. I have a picture-perfect memory and can recall just what you looked like in the early days, when you were a gofer for the old owner. I loved it when you came into your own and bought your first elegant business suit and stiletto heels, and sold your first really valuable work of art to a dear friend of mine. He still has it, by the way. He is another of your fans. You see, we don't have much on our minds when we get old, so we enjoy the simple pleasures – like following the career of a beautiful woman."

Dee listened intently, not sure yet whether she should be flattered or alarmed.

Then, in one fluid motion, Klaus placed his drink on the table, stood up, and, in an intimate gesture, delicately tucked a loose lock of Dee's hair behind her ear.

"Come, my lovely Dee, I would like to show you my art collection."

An hour later she had been through all of the rooms on the main floor of Klaus's triplex, the area he referred to as "the public rooms," although he rarely opened his home to anyone except his closest friends. Dee was feeling more comfortable alone in his presence, although, if she were forced to admit it to herself, she did find herself on guard. Against what, though, she wasn't sure. Klaus was without a doubt behaving like a gentleman, and treating Dee like a lady. And she was amazed at the size and beauty of his collection, which was composed almost in its entirety of portraits – and most of those were women. Dee had lost count as they wove through the maze of the elegantly-furnished suite of rooms that comprised the living room, the main dining room, a smaller dining room, the library, a music room, a study as well as several chambers that seemed to have no other purpose than to link the larger rooms and display more art.

At the end of one hall there was a private elevator, to which Klaus produced a key and invited Dee to step inside. Once again alarm bells rang in her head, and Klaus, seeing her hesitation, announced softly that they were about to see his most private collection.

Soft, indirect lighting gave the windowless room an eerie glow. Dee stood transfixed as she beheld seven of the most beautiful works of art she had ever seen. Without intending to, she gasped.

"Ah, my dear, I see that I have your attention now."

Dee remained speechless, staring at the canvas at the far end of the salon, which was surrounded by direct and indirect lighting that highlighted its ethereal beauty.

"I can see that she leaves you speechless, just as she does me, every time I see her. Is she not the loveliest lady?"

"Who, what is she, Klaus?" Dee finally said. She is 19th century and European, but why do I do not recognize her? Why do I not know this work?"

A chuckle escaped his lips. "She was painted by Giovanni Boldini when he was still in his youth, and, as you can see, he must have been madly in love with her."

"Of course," said Dee. "Boldini. His lines are so fluid, his colors clear, and the movements so sensual. But it is the artist's use of light that makes this painting so special – it appears to be almost translucent, doesn't it?"

Klaus nodded. "Later on he became more conformist, but in his youth he painted what he loved without the need to pander to paying clients."

"Oh, there is so much more to it than that, Klaus." She stopped for a moment and then decided to ask him the one question that was on her mind. "How do you come to have this painting in your possession?"

"It is rightfully mine, my dear. Do not worry about this one, although if I were brought to task I might have trouble with the provenance of one or two of the other ladies in this room. But, this one is mine by birthright. The lady in lace is my great-great-grandfather's youngest sister, and, while on vacation in Paris in the summer of 1867, the artist fell in love with her, painted her, and gifted her the canvas. Her name was Celeste."

Dee could not take her eyes off the painting, and stood transfixed even as Klaus told her the story. In the back of her mind was the thought that this painting had to be worth well over two million dollars – maybe even three.

"There is only one photograph in existence. A very long time ago, in Luxembourg, my grandfather invited a journalist in to view his collection, and the writer brought along his photographer. This same article has been reprinted several times since then, and every once in a while some art critic raises the question, 'Where is the Lady in Lace?' Was she lost during the war? Was she stolen from a museum?"

"And all this time, she has been here......" Dee's voice trailed off.

Klaus sighed deeply. "Yes, here, with me."

www.ingramcontent.com/pod-product-compliance
Lightning Source LLC
Chambersburg PA
CBHW020245150626
46552CB00020B/412